ACTIVIST

LOUISA REID

**GUPPY
BOOKS**

ACTIVIST
is a GUPPY BOOK

First published in the UK in 2022 by
Guppy Books,
Bracken Hill,
Cotswold Road,
Oxford OX2 9JG

Text copyright © Louisa Reid,
Cover and inside illustrations copyright © Yuzhen Cai

978 1 913101 74 9

1 3 5 7 9 10 8 6 4 2

Papers used by Guppy Books are from well-managed
forests and other responsible sources.

GUPPY PUBLISHING LTD Reg. No. 11565833

A CIP catalogue record for this book is available from the British Library.

Typeset in Gill Sans by Falcon Oast Graphic Art Ltd, www.falcon.uk.com
Printed and bound in Great Britain by CPI Books Ltd

There was only a quiet rain when they
       were dying;
   They must have heard the sparrows
       flying,
And the small creeping creatures in the
       earth where they were lying—
   But I, all day, I heard an angel crying:
   "Hurt not the trees."

'The Trees Are Down' by Charlotte Mew

PART ONE

NOW

SEPTEMBER

                                        with smiles,

                            our faces shine

                        bunches or braids,

                    black, pink, green –

                caught in the sun;

            brown and blonde,

        we burn,

    bright rivers of girls;

    red and gold,

We run,

RAINBOW

we are light

    striking water.

      We swallow wind,

        swell with fire,

          mouths full

            of beams

            and laughter,

          which we throw

              and catch

            and throw again

             to each another.

Dilly, Lori, Ria
and me.
Our names are

          atoms   exploding   colour,
and we are not the same
but we are everything to one another.

FIRST DAY

Here we come.
Gilded air greets us and
bows like a waiter
proffering knowledge
from a tempting silver spoon,
we pass manicured lawns,
and smiling teachers out to meet us.

I stop,
try to breathe,
here we go:
okay,   I can take it,   I *will* face it

and another school year begins.

TOWERS

Surrounding us:
walls.
Brick wrapped in ivy the red of old blood,
the flashing crimson of last year, the year before,
when I started to understand
the way things are here.

Why wouldn't Mum let me leave, go somewhere else?
The college in town? I could have got a bus,
ridden my bike,
but she worries, says, no –
it's too

dangerous.

I pause at the gates.
The woods call,
        the trees,
                the cradle of branches
where I have spent the summer
staring at the sky, trying to work out answers
to the questions my GCSE papers didn't ask.

SAME OLD

A brand-new form.
People I like, but also
people I don't.

They're all so loud,
going on about fancy holidays abroad
and who hooked up with who.
They leak mercury laughter, release pesticide smiles.

Dilly laughs, pulls a face, and nods.
"Yup, same old same old, I suppose."

PERIOD ONE

Maths and the relief of equations.
Unemotional, the page
demands my cool deliberation.

I try to lose myself in the work,
not to wrestle
with the knowledge of

binary systems
          and   gaping   holes.

I try to ignore the urgency of sunshine.
The clamour of fresh air.

I try to concentrate on
the possibilities here
(Mum's voice reminding me to
think of your future,
the doors wide open for you,
how lucky you are)
but there are whispers
as pens and pencils scratch at paper,
and phones flash under tables,
the distractions of
rifling pages.

Someone coughs,
and someone laughs.
Lori and I meet eyes.
I shake my head and get back to work.

TERRITORY

The bell rings for break and we rush
towards the common room,
shaking off yawns,
hugging friends we haven't seen for hours.

One lesson down. Four to go.
It smells musty,
and I can't touch the green of the day
or see myself walking across the ancient quad
out of here.
Music plays, cans hiss.
      I taste last chances and
                  something off.

We sit, a tangle of friends.
The look in Lori's eyes as she says,
"Shit, Cass, I missed you,
thank God you didn't leave and go to St Nick's –
for a while there we were worried,
weren't we, Ree?
Where've you been all summer anyway?"
She hugs me tight as if to prove it,
covering my cheeks and face with sloppy kisses.

Maria links my arm, agrees,
puts her head on my shoulder,
leaning in.
We claim a space
in the jungle of bodies, the chaos of noise.

CORDELIA

I look up.

Our corner
                is diagonally opposite from
                                their corner
but we try not to take any notice of
                the lads who whoop
                when Cordelia walks past
                coming to join us.
She flicks a finger, a perfect flash of disdain,
dodges snapping crocodile jaws,
moving fast and safe.

I sigh, we roll our eyes –

well, that's what worked this time last year
when we kept their nonsense
almost   quiet.

TREMORS

But something's going on this morning,
something's rumbling,
you can feel it in the hot glances,
a pulse that's quickening and rising.

What the hell is it now?
I can't be doing with their war.
Okay, here we go. It starts.

                                  God, I'm already tired.

READY

"What?" I call across the room,
(because that's what my friends expect –
that I'll speak up – and I guess I sound

the same, my voice as loud as it always was).
"What's up with you lot?"

It's Camilla who marches over,
swishy and sexy in her uniform
which is supposed to make us look
smart, not hot,
but she manages both
in a way I can't
and, quite frankly, don't want.
She looks me in the eye and says,
"Come on then, Cassandra. Admit it.
Was it one of you lot?"

"Was what us?"
I look at my mates,
we shrug and raise our eyebrows, and ask her
what the hell she's going on about.

AIM

Camilla shoves her phone under my nose
and a page reloads.

We gather, close
and read.

---

www.noshamenojudgement.com

*last summer after our GCSEs, i was at a party (you
know those parties, where there's drinking and drugs
and it's all so much) but I felt like shit. maybe my drink
was spiked, i dunno, but i remember staggering upstairs,
finding a bedroom on my own. i thought i'd be all right.
sleep it off, this awful feeling – i couldn't stand, or see,
my head aching and my blood so heavy like i was
almost dying or something. so i lay down for a bit.
sleep,
i thought,
i'll sleep.*

*and i must have passed out, cos the next thing i know,
i'm kind of awake, and someone's holding my arms,
while someone pulls down my shorts and shoves*

his fingers inside me.

and other things.

12

i wish i knew their names or the colour of their eyes, or their hair. but it was dark, and i was sick, like i said, with the drink and whatever, but they knew me. they knew who i was. said my name like i was just

dirt

i don't know how that could have happened to me.

i can't tell my friends, or my mum, or my dad, so here i am, telling you
anonymously
hoping people i don't know
might care

because right now i can't eat i can't sleep i can't breathe.

ANON Castle College

FIRE

My friends watch me.
Wait.
I push Camilla's phone away,
and quietly, seriously, I look her
dead in the eyes.
"Camilla – come on,
you know what it's like –
are you seriously saying
you're surprised?"

"Tell me," she says, her face flushing,
"who posted this pack of lies?"

"How the hell should I know?
And what makes you think it's not true?
Or that this has something to do with
one of your mates?
Enlighten us.
I mean, this post doesn't name names."

We stare, she blinks first, almost flinches
when I won't look away and I hold it, right there,
the challenge to decide
if she really wants to do this

with me,
right here.

Why doesn't she get
that the fact that
someone has had to post online
on an anonymous site
that she's been **drugged**
and **raped**
because there was **no one** to tell
because **no one** heard when we said
that the boys
treat the girls here
like meat
should be what's making her scream?

She knows I'm goading her, insinuating
something she doesn't want to accept,
but just as
I'm about to tell her
she needs to rethink her allegiances,
that her idea of feminism is seriously confusing me,
our phones ping,
unsolicited
notifications trill and twitter,

I stare at a message
flashed
and flashing
on my screen,

a picture of someone's
dick
cock
penis

whatever you want to call it,

unimpressive appendage, appallingly lit.

I hold up my phone, show the room
I'm not scared, shaking my head,
taking the piss.
What else can we do but mock
the state of it?
What would happen if we reported this?

"Come on, then," Lori shouts,
"which sad little man
thinks this is cute?"

But the game here isn't to make us laugh,

it's to make us scared.
That's what gets me,
that's what makes me
too impatient
to wait for some authority
to act and reassure me
that it's okay, a one-off, they're good guys really
and we ought not get so

mad.

WE RISE

I don't recognise the account
but I know the style
of the next photo – even more pornographic,
        utterly vile.

So I get up and go,
                over to their side
                                of the room,
        swallowing bile and
        armed with disgust,
        a weapon that only fires   so far   but is all
                                        I've got.

"You know what, Jamie Jenkins, you're completely gross,"
I snarl into his face,
"and I'm going to show this screenshot to the police
on the day you get arrested,
as I'm sure you will,
for being an actual pervert
whose brain,
   – if he has one,
              and that's up for debate –
is currently lodged somewhere between his legs."

His friends are watching, creasing up and
howling with the comedy
of harassing us,

                    at me
                    standing there
                    trying to convince them
                    that they
                    Just. Aren't. Funny.

Jamie's grin is wide and white,
body spasming at how
hilarious he thinks he is.

"Who says I sent that?" he laughs
"Like, you can prove it, right?"

I stab a finger in his direction.

"Did you even read that post?
Don't you give a shit about that girl?
She's one of us.
Someone here, in this school,
maybe in this room,
and all you can do is take the piss?
What's wrong with you, Jamie?
Why are you being like this?"

"CALM DOWN, LOVE,"

Henry says, from the windowsill where he's perched,
watching the show,
sipping a coffee, idly eating toast.
Jamie's best friend
and my friend, once, too.

I look at him.
Try to pose the question with my eyes:
Why are you so awful now?

But before it can really kick off,
there's a hand on my arm,
Mo, and beside him, Simeon and Luke –
nice boys there with the apologies
and *ignore hims* and
he's a wanker,
Mo even trying to pull me into a hug,
but I see the ones who are keeping quiet.

I guess it's hard
to be a traitor, to refuse to play the game,
and I watch them

                liminally   drifting,

allegiance   switching

from us   to them

                         and back again.

These are the boys
we went to nursery school with.
Our mums share memories
of lost teeth, sunny days and sweet dreams.

These are the boys
who fell in love with us then
and wrote sweet messages in halting pencil,

misspelling our names and their own,
littering their notes with wavering kisses.

Their fingerprints blurred with ours
on monkey bars,
they stepped in our footsteps in the sandpit
and we were messy and muddy
and pure together.

These are the boys
we raced,
tied at our ankles,
three-legged friends.

These are the boys we loved,
in the way you love yourself
when you're too young to understand
all the ways
the world will make you change.

THEN

LESSON ONE

When we first started at Castle College,
two years ago,
in Year Ten when our schools merged,
blending boys and girls,
they said,
Welcome!
A new era awaits!
It'll do the boys good to have you
young ladies around!

Ladies?
Er, since when?
I didn't like that word, even then.
And I didn't realise
these boys needed
girls like us to
tame them.
What was this?
Were we here
to dilute their testosterone
with some of our soothing oestrogen?

LESSON TWO

"So, the powers that be
have requested that we
field a mixed debate team
this year to cement our commitment to,
            ahem,

                        diversity,"
Sir said, back then, that very first term,
his wry eyebrow and sardonic laugh
setting off titters amongst the boys.

Deputy Head, Mr Sheen, called the shots,
head tilted so far back
            he looked down his nose as
                        he surveyed us – poor little sods,
shiny with hope, fresh and new,
we were up for anything,
so desperate to please them and to do well.

The teacher lasered our faces,
peering over the top of his glasses,
mouth twitching with the effort
of supressing his derision.

"So which one of you young ladies

wants to take their chance?
Let's see what you're made of, yes?
Come on. Don't all shout at once."

Sir, as he preferred to be called,
liked to swoop around the classroom in his gown.
Old-school – he preferred things
as they had been once
upon
a very long
time ago.
There's nothing wrong with the status quo,
he was fond of saying,
now then, dear, let's not cause a row.
And so, since everyone was waiting,
I stood up
because, let's face it, who else would?

"I'll do it,"
I said, legs trembling under the desk,
and the class whooped
and someone jeered
and someone said,
"Big Mouth strikes again."
Aged fourteen and scared
I was out of my depth,

I smiled and
told Sir that I couldn't wait.

LESSON THREE

Henry.
Leader of innumerable packs
and every teacher's favourite
charming young man
sat next to me at lunch
and introduced his best mate –
Jamie,
who instantly
asked Dilly out.

LESSON FOUR

Jamie followed us around like an annoying smell.
He showed me his list
in biology, the second week of term,

as I worked:
a pig's heart on the bench before me.

"Right, Cassie," he said,
"so, you're ranked and rated – look –
this is what you've got:
your tits are a two
and your legs are an eight."

"Oh, right, cheers," I said, feeling the heat,
the scalpel twitching sharp in my fingers,
                              "and, tell me, Jamie, erm,
                                    any thoughts on
                                        my brain?"

He laughed. "What? That's irrelevant."

And before I knew what else to say,
Henry chimed in, quirking an eyebrow,
shaking his head.
"Hang on now, Jimbo,
could we show a little more respect?"
But Jamie just grinned
and flourished his league table under my nose.

Their date was
awks,
Dilly said, she had no idea why she even went.
Jamie was a groper,
                his hands moved
                                like spiders or crabs
and it made her feel
kind of gross
            to be grabbed
                        and poked
                                    about.

LET BATTLE COMMENCE

"The motion is," Sir said, as we began the prep,
"that this house would rather have
a government of experts
than one which is
democratically elected."
Henry nodded, thinking, and responded first.
"Interesting. Nice challenge.
And we get to propose?
Fantastic stuff."

I thought it was dry and dusty,
but when I remembered what Dilly's mum had told
    me,
about how the whole idea of democracy
had been undermined –
that 'rule by the people'
no longer meant
that anyone was listening
to what the people actually wanted,
how the government was actually moving
to remove our rights – the chance to noisily protest –
I began to see
how this could work.

"There's a problem with representation
when a referendum
can ignore half the population," I told Henry,
who tapped his pen on his teeth, and wrote down the
    point,
"especially whilst they're so unrepentant
about the damage that they've done
to health and education,
public services,
I mean their stance on taxation
surely can't be what the majority want?"

The more I researched,
the more I realised that I could nail this.
Mum had always said I talked too much
and here was my chance to prove her wrong.
Words were good, right?
Mightier than any sword.
That's what Grandad said when me and my brother
    fought.

Henry smiled, threw his pen in the air, caught it,
and watched me, watching him.
"You know, Cassie, you're really not bad at all."
We were in the library and he leaned in, whispered
his next words, moving his head close to mine.
"And you're actually quite fit
when you get all fired up.
Who gives a shit where you're ranked?"

I shoved him
and he laughed and so did I,
just to show I knew it was a joke,
I told myself that he was teasing me
like my stupid brother would.

We practised our speeches,
late nights at his house, and I gave back

as good as I got, more besides.

In those days there was only an inch
between us in height, before he shot up,
back then, Year Ten,
when I could meet his eyes.

ONE OF THE GANG

Henry told his mates that I was
formidable, leaning back in his chair in the form room,
feet up on the desk.
Barely fourteen and already
judge and jury of the popular people.

Henry looked into my eyes and smiled.
I blushed when
everyone looked at me
with something like respect.

WINNING

Whip smart, we could parry phrases,
dance around our opponents
with tongues like rapiers.

In the first round Henry and I sliced our way to
    victory.
He grabbed my shoulders afterwards
as the hall emptied
and hugged me, saying,
"Cassandra, you're a legend."
I laughed, face hot, still trembling, and said,
"All right, calm down."
But Henry loved our success
and how viciously I could dismantle
a spurious argument.

His mum laughed at us,
called us the little dictionaries
and we'd text each other new words.
He told me I was *audacious*,
I told him to quit the *persiflage*.

VICTORY

Before the final I was shaking
but Henry squeezed my hand
and said in a low, determined voice,
"We've got this, Cassie, it's a walk-over –
have you seen the state of that pair?
State school standard.
Literally no contest whatsoever."
And he was right. We won.

We posed for photos, for the school website
and the local paper,
waving our trophy aloft,
each with a hand on its gleaming glory,
Sir even smiled at me and said,
"Congratulations, Cassandra,
I think you rather proved yourself."

NOW

HATE

I hate the way things have changed.
Why couldn't we all have just stayed friends?
And I hate how my rage has taken shape,
is faithful,
like a dog
that sits at my feet,
snarling.
I know it well, can muzzle it
when I need to,
will feed it when it growls.
It follows me for the rest of the day,
sits beside me,
heavy tail thumping
a beat that is as familiar as my heart.

THE GIRLS

After school I wait by the gate.
The stones of the school are warm.

33

I drop my shoulders for the first time all day,
breathe out

                              a huge sigh.

Lori's first:
longest legs, loudest laugh.
"Nice work," she says.
She means the way I stood up to Jamie, I guess.

"Sure. But look, what are we going to do about them?"
I ask as Ria catches up, Dilly next.

"Wish I knew," she says.

We walk towards the woods,
our place of dens and dreams,
and sit to watch the sun sing through the leaves, still
    green,
last chorus of summer on its lips,
time halting as we wait
and wonder:
what's next?

"Who was it?" Maria asks.
"The girl who left that post online?
What party do you reckon she meant?

The one at Camilla's? Luke's?
God, they were practically every night."

Yes, who is she?
The girl who's been brave enough
to spill her pain
to offer it up
and get us all to face up
to the thing people wish we'd accept
as part of our biological inheritance.

Shit, she's got guts.
Or maybe she's just done with keeping quiet.

INTERRUPTIONS

Noise drifts on the breeze,
shifting the air.

The playing fields are so close we can almost smell
the competition, taste the sweat
of boys charging down the pitch,
rugby ball tight in their grip.

I close my eyes,
see Henry there,

the grinning sweaty selfie
that pollutes his Insta every week,
the wolfish teeth.
I bet he stinks.

QUESTIONS

Dilly sits and stares into space.
She shakes her head and stretches up to the sky,
long hair, big blue eyes, dimples and
an optimist's smile.
She points at a branch –
"Look, up there."
I follow the line of her arm, see the bird, poised,
territorial and suspicious, beady eyes.
"What is it?" Dilly asks
and I name the
Great Grey Shrike,
definitive for its hooked bill and slate grey back.
A rare bird,

it impales prey on thorns,
the better to get at their fleshy insides.

I watch Dilly. Wonder.
Would she keep it from us if she'd been hurt?
I think she'd share it, that she wouldn't be ashamed.
Maria is the quiet one,
who'd try to smother her pain
in case it hurt someone else.
I look at my friend with the biggest brown eyes
softest skin and dark hair
and try to speak without words,
like I'm saying,
Come on, Ria,
you can tell us, if you like.

She blinks once, twice,
and I squeeze her hand,
look back at Cordelia.
"So, what do we think, Dills?
Any ideas?"

"No clue.
Do you think it was Jamie? One of their group?
I mean, it's their kind of move."

"Maybe, I dunno."

"Well, something has to happen, right?
We can't ignore this.
Cass? Have you got a plan? Or what?'

We watch our phones, reload the page,
and the posts
multiply,

it seems that word's got round
that finally there's a place for
anonymous voices to tell their stories,

where the naming
and shaming
is directed not at victims
but at perpetrators,
the schools and colleges,
even universities,

there's a place
for those girls
who want to stop being ignored.

And it is the woods who whisper their support,

it is the wind in the leaves,
the last sun,
that catches and stirs our resolve.

SEE YOU TOMORROW

We run –
      race,
            rage in flames,
                  out of the woods and
                        into the waiting world.

We rise
        we swell
                we soar
                      and paint the sky –

Clouds part as
we swallow time
and fill black holes with fire.

Watch us burn.
We are elemental –

Impossible
Unstoppable
Girls.

PART TWO

NOW

KICKING OFF

By teatime my mum's phone is full of
WhatsApp messages,
mums and dads with daughters
or sons,
who've seen the website and
want to know
where the school's gone wrong.

**I'm not paying 20K a year for my daughter to be
treated like a piece of meat**

my son's no rapist
he's a good boy – you can't tar them all
with the same brush

yes but –

**It's not my boy; he's been taught better than
    that.**

Come on, don't you think
some of these girls are being hysterical?

43

It's a witch hunt! Pure misandry run wild.
I'm going to write to the Head
things were all right before she came along.

They should never have let the girls in.
Castle College is a boys' school.
We should have seen this coming.

Good God! Dr March has done nothing wrong!
This problem didn't arrive with her.

Rubbish! I find her politics utterly abhorrent.

Your girls need to know how to cope
with the real world.

No they don't!

It's carnage.
Mum switches off and won't answer when I ask her
what she plans to do, but her teeth are set
in a grimace that makes me wonder
if today's the day
she finally wakes up.

MY MOTHER

wouldn't call herself a feminist.
If you asked her
she'd say
she believes in keeping the peace,
to knuckling down and getting on with things.

And yes, I agree, that peace is great
in theory, but
                    looked at slant, it's just an excuse
                    to turn the other cheek.

PUSHOVER

I'm in bed, and Mum's awake
downstairs on her own.
There is a loneliness about my mother's life
that I'm not sure she likes
even though she says
it's preferable to the other
lives she could have had
(meaning with my dad, who is somewhere

far from here,
travelling to dangerous places,
changing the world with his
photographs of suffering and war,
which I see on the news and
I keep in a book
as documentary evidence that he exists).

Mum tells people,
as she rolls her eyes, that:
"Cassie would like me to set the world on fire,"
and smiles in a way that says
she doesn't find it funny at all.

Dilly's mum laughed when she overheard and said,
"Come on, Donna,
you are more powerful than you know."
But my mum just shrugged
and drank her prosecco
like it was a panacea for all ills.

I go downstairs to find her
sitting typing an email to my school,
I watch as she reads it through,
spellcheck,
grammar check

then
delete
and start again.
"You're the one with all the words, Cass," she sighs,
"tell me what to put.
It's just dreadful, this furore. I haven't a clue."

She wishes I wouldn't shout,
wishes I wouldn't
think the worst of her for
preferring quiet,
for calling my father's job
a waste of a life.

I retype the questions, the queries:
*"What exactly does the school plan to do to protect my
    daughter?"*
and find my mother's voice for her.
She sighs again and says,
"Since when did anything either of us thinks
make a difference in this world?"
Then presses send.

UTOPIA

Our head, Dr March,
has been trying, bless her, ever since she joined
the staff, to raise our voices.
She wants us to feel like we belong
as much as she wishes she did.

But now her approval rating is at an all-time low
and she knows she's got something to prove:
we're girls in a boys' school,
will be women in male spaces.
And you know, men
don't like to have their toes
stepped on.
They prefer their feet firmly planted
deep in the soil,
stretched and spreading, roots like wire.

So, she wants us all doing STEM,
thinks that's the way to show we're fully prepared:
that we can compete in a world where ability counts
more than the gender we were designated at birth.
She wants us ambitious and smart,
debating and fighting for our right to be heard,
        leaning in.

Her first words
to us were:

"There are no limits to what we can achieve
if we work as a team.
We'll make this school a crucible of knowledge
where you, the young people of the future,
will flourish in a place of true equality."

I remember the speech.
My spirit stirred
and I thought,
Yes! Of course!
She made it sound so simple, so right.

But then, in physics
that first day,
when I sat with my hand up
until I put my hand down
because it ached
with the effort of waiting
to be noticed,

I began to wonder.

RECONCILIATION

Old Sheeny marches into the common room,
and silences the talk of weekend plans,
the Friday feeling that we're almost nearly free again.
"Break's cut short.
Get down to the hall."

"What the hell?" I look at Dilly,
she shrugs.
"Emergency assembly," the Deputy Head shouts,
"let's move along fast."

It must be because it hasn't stopped.
All week the evidence has been piling so high
that the website's almost buckled
under the weight
of testimony
from almost every school in the country,
detailing the way girls have been
systematically abused,
and after our school was named
and shamed
last night
on the local news,
I'll bet Dr March is panicking

and thinks that since we've been treated like pieces of
    meat,
it will be a great idea
to bring us all together and confront this pain,
spread it all out:
a buffet of despair.

Maybe that will make it all go away.

ASSEMBLED

We file into the hall,
everybody grumbling as
they take their places in the
huge space
observed by portraits of austere faces,
grim ghosts of the past,
industrialists, economists,
even a long-dead prime minister –
livid at the damage being done
to the reputation of their alma mater.

We line up, as directed.

"Girls facing boys," Dr March instructs
as she watches from the platform at the front of the
    hall.

Our teachers flank the rows
marshalling us into orderly lines
and no one dares speak

yet.

But there are sighs
and stares.
I nudge Dilly, whisper,
"Just look at us, one big happy family,
what a load of crap, what do you reckon's up?"

Dr March catches my eye, glares, and announces,
"This is a restorative assembly,
a chance to show we can and will do better."

Henry looks at me long and hard
then shakes his head.
I hold up my hands in a gesture that means:
What? You think I did this?

ATTENTION

We stand in rows,
tried to rape us.
they thought
disgusting
to stop their friends
their fingers
have laughed and
like a trophy.

face the faces
We face the boys
treating us like that
but didn't have
sticking their hands
inside our bodies
shared
A football.

who might have
who said
was violating
the guts
into our clothes
They might even
the evidence
Or a bag of chips.

SYMBOLISM

The boys are told
to approach us
one by one
and apologize for hurting us –

                    whether they are guilty or not.

"It's a gesture of solidarity,"
Dr March says,
severe in her expensive cream suit
and skyscraper heels that indent the wooden floors,

53

as she paces the rows,
marking the hall with her resolve.

"After this we can all start afresh;
put the past behind us,
face the future
and each other
with a new respect."

I wonder if she's got the press
lurking somewhere, snapping pictures –
documenting a new era
where misogyny is dead.

DISRUPT

"Dr March,"
I call over the racket,
just as things are getting started
and Eli Abraham in Year Eleven,
who wouldn't say boo to a butterfly,
is shuffling up to be the first to
ask us to forgive him,

hands shoved deep in his pockets,
his cheeks fiery with embarrassment –
as fiery as his hair –
his eyes on the floor.
I step out of my row.

"Dr March," I repeat.

"Not now, Cassandra,
see me after assembly if you wish."
Her dismissal signalled by a
twitch of an eye, the decisive swivel of a heel.

I move so she has to see me, hear me.

"No," I tell her, loudly.
"This is a joke.
I won't participate in this charade
that treats innocence
like guilt
and suggests guilt is
a matter of no consequence."

She holds up a hand,
so I turn and walk back amongst the rows.
"Come on," I say, stopping Eli in his tracks,

smiling and nodding him towards the exit,
"they can't make you do this. Let's go."

"Cassandra. Stay where you are," commands the
    Headteacher.

"No way. I'm sorry, but you've got this all wrong."

A snort.
I swivel and look Henry in the eye.

"Let's just be clear,"
I say, my voice bouncing
        from the high ceiling
to the floor,
                and up against the walls,
"you're not going to get me forgiving
anyone
anytime soon,
not until I know
that this isn't just for show
and that the perpetrators, whoever they may be,
have been properly punished.
I'm not going to be part of something
where the good are humiliated
and the bad get away with it."

I stab a finger at the boys, then at the Head.
"If.   there.   are.   rapists.   in.   our.   school,
shouldn't someone be calling the police?"

There is no answer from
the Headteacher
or her esteemed Deputy
(whose face is turning the colour of over-cooked ham)
or anyone else
and so
I march towards the door,
dragging Eli with me,
despite the teachers lining up
and telling me to stop, think again,
and to just, for heaven's sake, cooperate

                                        for once.

Dilly hurries to my side and we link arms,
turn around,
wait and watch as Lori summons
an exodus
of girls.

There's muttering and then the murmurs grow
to nervous laughter
that drowns out the teachers' imprecations

to stay where you are, be quiet and show some
    respect.
Camilla stares and then shrugs,
rolls her eyes
and joins our tribe when she sees her friends
coming over to our side.

But before we're even halfway free, Henry's
                    pushing past, the tip
                        of a tornado
                        of boys,
                            who
            hurl through the mass of us with
    shoulders   squared   and   voices
                        raised.
            "Sod this, it's bullshit, this is
                    misandry,"
                    they yell

and I watch them run,
trampling the truth
as they go.

SUMMONED

"Insurrection is inappropriate in these circumstances."

"But Dr March—"

"Enough. I understand emotions are running high
but nothing excuses insolence of the kind
you expressed today."

"But Dr March—"

"It's not your place to question my authority.
I have no choice but to send you home.
And I will expect a sincere written apology."

"But Dr March—"

"Cassandra. Enough.
Your grandfather is on his way to pick you up."

GRANDAD

doesn't say much. An eyebrow raised
at the suggestion that we don't tell my mum.

"Why did you get me in the car?
I could have walked."

He sighs. Chuckles. Says he was in a rush
and forgot to think about his carbon footprint –
he was dealing with his granddaughter
who's old enough to know better.

Silence.
He chuckles again,
tells me I'm nothing like my mum.

"She was a quiet one, you know,
when she was at school.
Always has been, really.
You must get it from your dad.
What do they say, these days,
no filter?
That's your problem, Cassie."

"Problem?"

"Well, yes, it could end in more trouble than you
    think."

I roll my eyes.
"Didn't you know, Trouble's my middle name?"

"Oh, come on, smile –
it's not as bad as all that.
Let's go for an ice cream."

"Actually, Grandad, it's worse.
Can you let me out here, please, I want to walk?"

We're passing the woods and I want to
run, scream, escape
and curse at the state of everything,
even him
with his well-meaning words,
his treats and twinkling smiles
and easy dismissal of everything I care about.

I need to go and bathe in the trees
bury my feet
deep in the earth,
ground myself
away from the noise.

"Cassie, just to remind you, and I don't mean
to sound like an old fart,
but you are in Lower Sixth,
maybe you should be going home
and actually doing some work?"

We stop at the lights and I open the door,
ignore him
and go.

BUT

Where there should be peace and quiet,
open air,
there is a convoy of lorries, and
a gang of men.
I run to see what's going on,
and stare up at the hoarding, the monstrous billboard
that reads:
Elysian Fields.

They're hauling their barriers and blockades,
erecting hideous plastic fences,

cordoning off nature.
Blokes who whistle and holler from one to another,
and don't see me
or the wildflowers they're trampling,
or the birds who are flying,
startled into the air.
I turn back to face Grandad who's pulled up beside
    me.
"What the hell?" I howl. "Did you know about this?"

Grandad rolls down the window of
his ancient sporty MG
and shakes his head.
"Come on, Cassie, get back in.
Let's go home.
We'll find out what's going on."

"Have you seen the state of it, Grandad?
I gesture at the 3D mock-up of so-called paradise
and chuck   a handful of dust   into the sky.

MOTHER EARTH

Of course, she's theirs to exploit,
to mine and frack and rip

a	part
split	open
de	stroy.

I load the website on my phone
as Grandad drives and I talk, competing with
the crackle of Classic FM.
"I can't believe this.
They reckon they're going to pull down our wood—"
Ancient oaks,
homes of birds and insects and adventure.
Rare red squirrels and tiny creatures,
invisible to the naked eye,
that crawl and perch
and exist.

These are the trees I've sheltered in,
cradles, nests;
trees where I once
built imaginary worlds out of leaves and twigs,
the bones of the earth; my bones, too.

Our woods smell of secrets and summer,
their dirt is ingrained into my hands and feet,
the smell of it is deep in my hair,
my trees, our trees,
the trees that breathe for us.
Ancient things.

They want to pull down our trees and shove up flats,
high-rise apartments for more millionaires.
Concrete and glass, prestigious prisons for the myopic
whose vision stretches
no further than their screens.

Not on my watch.
No flipping way.

COMFORT

Grandad drives me back to his bungalow
and Grannie feeds me on the
vegan ice cream and brownies she keeps especially
for days like this.

I swear. A lot.
Then tell them everything that's been going on
at school.
They stare at me, appalled
at the stories that girls have spilled,
but then Grannie says,
"I'm sad to say,
I'm not surprised. This is typical, Cassie.
It's been the lot of all women from time immemorial
but I'm afraid your generation
is facing the worst."

"So what do we do?"

She has no answers.
I look at my grandad,
"Come on, you're a man, tell me,
how do we make them realize
we're human, too?"
And the old man frowns,
as impotent
as me.

THEN

SOMETHING TO PROVE

Grandad used to drop me at school.
He'd get out of the car and wave me off,
watching until I disappeared.
I know because I'd look back, just one last
glance to check
he was there,
a safe, still point in a turning world.

I used to call him every night when I got home
to tell him what I'd learnt that day
and I could hear his smile when he replied.

He loved the fact I wasn't afraid to debate.
"Cassie, you're a clever thing, we're so proud of you,
your grannie and me.
Let us know when the competition's on."

I didn't tell him
that standing up there in front of all those eyes
was actually
my worst nightmare,
because if I failed

or
said something wrong,
it wouldn't just be myself that I was letting down.

NOW

THE TRUTH OF THE MATTER

"What on earth's going on?
Why did the school call Grandad
 and demand he take you home?
Who have you been rude to now?"

Mum comes home at last, full of hot air.
Of course, it's my fault,
it's always my fault.
She chucks down her bag, her coat
and sticks her hands on her hips.

"Don't you even care, Mum?
Did you hear what they made us do at school today?
Or are you just going to blame me for everything
    again?"

"What are you talking about?"

"It's war. I mean it,
on two fronts.
They're not pulling down my trees
and I'm not going to sit back and shut up."

I show her the website again,
share the proof that it's not just me being difficult,
on one of my missions to change the world;
that there are so many of us,
so many of us,
that victims won't suffer in silence any more.

"So yeah, I admit it, I kicked off a bit with Dr March,
but she wants us all to just 'reconcile'
and start afresh,
but the boys, actually, some of them are practically
    men,
well, they can't just be allowed to carry on –
the culture's toxic. So vile.
So I told her to shove it,
all her rubbish about forgiveness,
and fresh starts.
Whatever, Henry was way ruder than me.
He'd better have been sent home as well."

Why am I not surprised when Mum tells me not to
    rock the boat?
That Henry isn't as bad as I make out.
That she saw his mum in Waitrose the other night and
    she said
how sad it was that we weren't still friends

and wondered if we might not all go round for supper
    one of these days.

"She can stick her supper
up her arse," I say.

Why am I not surprised when Mum implies
I'm over-reacting?
Why am I not surprised when she asks
if maybe
we're exaggerating the threat?
If my wokeness hasn't got a little bit
out of hand?

"Has anyone ever interfered with you, Cassie?"
she says.

My brother appears in the kitchen,
where I'm standing open-mouthed,
lost for words, for once,
and rolls his eyes and his joint.
"Mum. That's not the point."
I nod. Close my eyes. Breathe.
At least someone gets it,
even if he is half asleep,
too much weed
dulling him into a perpetual dream.

PART THREE

NOW

SEPTEMBER

MISSION POSSIBLE

I throw on my uniform and Mum off the scent,
yelling goodbye as I
slam the front door and head out.

We've been plotting.
Weeks of outrage growing, like vines, winding,
binding us together in decision.

A protest at the woods,
my idea,
that with Grandad's help
we got the Greens to support.

We have the power,
we have voices, words,
we can scream and shout
for the creatures, the bees, and beetles, spiders and snails,
the tiny insects that can't speak for themselves.

A car beeps, I jump
and stick two fingers up
at the guy who's leering – old and sad –
tongue hanging out like a slobbering dog
at me
in my school uniform.

I grab my phone,
hold it up to capture his number plate,
and walk backwards holding his eyes with mine,
mouthing all the reasons
he should be ashamed of himself.
You dirty old man.
I flip my fingers in a sign that means
fuck you, creep,
and he grins and beeps again
before speeding away.

READY

At Dilly's I get changed into
trainers, T-shirt dyed in purple, white and green
and emblazoned with our motto:
DO NOT TOUCH

on my front

HANDS OFF

on my back.

The message should be clear enough.

Dilly's mum joins us,
hugs me and says,
"Ready?"
She doesn't care that we're skipping school —
she lit the fire inside me when I was ten,
when we marched against the government,
Dilly and I walking behind, holding hands,
in awe of her voice, megaphone loud,
amplified, reverberating,
a wild woman on the rampage.
She caught my eye, and winked,
leaned towards me and said,
"Never be afraid to speak up, Cassie, okay?"

Moira and Jack were Dad's friends really.
Mum hadn't wanted me to go,
but on the train home from London that day,
Moira encouraged us to rail

against injustice,
and the plight
of people in countries far from ours;
she explained how our leaders
traded with monsters,
and sold guns to dictators,
supplying weapons to genocidal maniacs
and put gold before good –
she said we should care about everyone's mess,
not just the tip in our own backyard.

And when a man sitting in the seat across the aisle said,
"For Christ's sake,
would you give it a rest?"
she looked at him,
and laughed and told him,
"I'll rest when I'm dead,"
and offered him a Jaffa Cake.

INSPIRATION

Dilly used to go bright red
when Moira got talking.
I think she was embarrassed by her mum's

hippy clothes, dancing bangles,
hands full of rings and her dyed bright pink hair –
handbag full of homemade snacks and sweets –
but I actually think she's the coolest woman
I've ever met.

Today we carry banners, and streamers,
and wave our smiles
as we walk towards the woods
that hover behind school.

We march into the swell of purpose,
exhilaration pulling us tall,
and I turn to my friends,
we link arms, connected, safe,
and we talktalktalk, all the way,
tireless talk of everything we can still do,
and still become.

WORDS NOT DEEDS

"So, what I think, right, is
that we need to start something,
something big.

And this is the beginning,
isn't it?" I say to Moira, who nods,
egging me on, and together
we scream at cars as they pass,
and raise our chant:

DO NOT TOUCH!
HURT NOT THE TREES!

No one stops, though they slow
to gawp and laugh
and some bloke yells,
"What's this? Day trip from the loony bin?"

To them we're just a cluster of schoolies,
teenage girls and weirdos,
mums with babies in buggies,
grandads and grannies, folk in green anoraks
making a nuisance, causing a racket.

I chase a car down the road,
pelt them with the missiles
they threw first.

They want to pull down our woods,
so we'll pull down their signs.

"Let's go," I say,
panting, hands on hips and trying to breathe
slower,
to calm down,
but my heart is racing with this –
the anger,
and a fear that I feel like a feral thing,
that unless we fight,
everything I love will disappear.

A guy with dreads hands me a rope
that he's looped over one of the poles
and the girls line up behind me
and we pull, and pull and pull, a tug of war,
until the billboard topples, crashing into the road.

I Snapchat, Insta, tweet and text,
we dance
in sync – post it fast –
urging more people to join us:
the bigger we are the better.

We jump on the fallen sign,
stamp holes in the grins of those automatons
who advertise this crime as if it's something that
    should make us smile.

All I can hear is my laughter,
the noise that comes from my belly,
and erupts out of my throat.
It helps.
It means that I'm alive,
right?

STRENGTH

At lunchtime our numbers swell.
Grannie and Grandad show up with flasks of
    vegetable soup,
bars of chocolate, and cheering words
as the kids from our year and the years below
sneak out through the hole in the fence
at the back of the playing fields
and we're louder, noisier than ever,
banging drums and blowing whistles.
Moira shouts down her megaphone,
lectures on the climate crisis,
screams about the danger
of believing humankind is the superior species.

I tell the newcomers to stay and listen,
that this is real education.
I round people up, grab hands, offer thanks,
tell them not to bother with afternoon school.
We sit and our bodies barricade the road.
See us?
We.   will.   not.   be.   moved.

RUMBLE

Ria's playing her guitar.
She sings of how we are candles,
little fires,
the beginning of a conflagration.

Lori harmonizes,
she has a voice like liquid thunder,
like her heroes, Nina and Ella.
She grins when she meets my eyes
as if she can feel the extraordinary fire,
the energy, the love
that's here.

The sun's shining, and
possibilities smoulder, my heart beats stronger.
Where there are fifty, sixty kids
singing together,
isn't that hope?
I lift my voice, sing louder, make more noise.

But the sound of engines revving, horns beeping,
wheels screeching
intrudes.

It's Henry and Jamie and Marcus and their mates
from the year above
in their brand-new posh boy cars,
tests just passed.
They squeal to a halt, engines belching fumes
and tyres burning rubber,
leaning on their horns.

They're not here to help.

Plastic bottles, litter, crap
pelted
at us.

Engines rev,

as
they
edge
their
cars
up
too
close
so we can
smell
the stench
of diesel,
the burning
oil.
Thick
heavy
fumes
pollute the
air.

"Fuck off," I yell,
as
hard plastic
and metal,
a heavy
weight,

lands in my back.
I dig in my heels, trying to get a grip
    on the road
        as the engine screams and there's
           a little nudge,
            a shove,
                that shunts me forward,
                    down onto the tarmac.

COWARDS

I'm screaming and swearing again,
turning to see Henry's face, splitting with laughter,
as I'm scraping at the road with my nails,
    my friends grabbing my shoulders,
        holding on,
until they finally reverse and
speed away, up the lane.

I stand up,
and howl
into the air behind them.

Dilly pulls me close, arm around my waist.
"Ignore them, Cassie, come on, don't let them wind
    you up –
don't get so upset, that's what they want."

But I'm crying, can't help it, sob out the words,
"I hate them, though, Dilly,
they're the epitome of everything that sucks."

I gesture towards school.
"And that place, I mean, what a joke.
Absolutely nothing's been done.
They think it's all just gone away.
I'm going to speak to Ms Lark,
see if she'll support us,
I reckon she will.
We've got to do something about them,
what about a petition?
At least that would be a start?"

Lori agrees, wrapping her arms around us both.
We form a line across the road, arms linked in
    solidarity.

We shouldn't have to wonder when
we'll be cut

down
to size,
we shouldn't have to
anticipate our steps in the dark,
     how to dodge the hands,
negotiate our
        survival.

It runs along our bodies, vibrations of fear
speaking silent volumes
because we get it,
all of us know
a girl who
won't come to school
       because a boy in her form
       won't leave her alone.
We all dread
the picture someone might take while we're
waiting for the bus, or just out with our friends,
stuck on a naked body, legs wide apart,
then shared with his mates,
then shared with
the world.

We could all be the girl who cries herself to sleep
because no one believes her when she says she hurts.

Who's been told
that what happened to her wasn't really rape.

All the girls silently suffering
and blaming themselves
for something that is never their fault.

But we'll fix this, I swear,
Dilly and Lori and Ria and me.
Our voices shake the sky.
We watch the clouds rattle and the rain retreat –
we will not be silenced,
we will send a message that
the people, we the people, will be heard.

Don't touch us,
I scream into the sun.

INTERFERENCE

My phone vibrates,
cross in my pocket,
I don't answer, know it will be Mum,

she always wants to know
things.
Like who I'm with,
when I'll be home,
and if I'm safe,
why the hell I'm not at school.

But I don't need the blessing of
institutions designed to cage me,
turn me out as just another cog in their machine,
another rat running the race,
driven by greed.

What will be the point in knowing French verbs
if there is no world left to conjugate?
What will be the point in understanding atoms
if our planet has exploded?

My phone buzzes again, irate –
so many missed calls,
I want to throw it into the nearest rubbish bin –
but I listen to the message,
Mum pleading,
What are you up to now?
She literally won't give up
so I text, only to say I'll be home late,

shove my phone to the bottom of my bag,
push back into the fray and   leap onto a

                                                              fallen log,

wave my arms,
wave my words
into the face of the waiting world.

I am a flag-flying
Lie-defying
Freedom-fighting
Activist.

MOVE ALONG, PLEASE

The police insist
it's time to stop,
moving among us,
loud and certain that
enough is enough.
"None of you kids should be down here,
you should be in school.
Clear off before we take you down to the station.
You're disrupting the traffic, we've got residents
    complaining."

Others aren't so lucky, the dreadlocked guy
is being questioned, and
Dilly's mum is being manhandled
into the back of a police van
whilst we're corralled towards town,
and told not to come back.

SO NOT DONE

At Dilly's place, later, we gather
round Moira,
curse the police and the corporations.
"Girls," she says, "this is serious."
She picks up her phone, and begins to call
people who she intends to enlist
in our fight against this.
"We don't back down.
We fight back," she says.
If anyone can mobilize an army
this woman will.

She waves us away, and we go upstairs to Dilly's room,
splice together footage, edit our message.

I post a photo on my Instagram page,
black and white –
me, and Dilly, faces bright with rage,
tag my dad
and hope he might at least see
that I'm doing my best.

But I can't stop thinking about Henry.
Henry in that car,
Henry laughing and sneering and thinking he's
won.
"So, listen, right, I've been thinking.
We have to do something at school.
We want to be safe, need to make them change,
we can't just bury what's gone on.
This petition idea.
What do you reckon?
Should we make a start?
Put forward some demands?"

We run it by Dilly's dad,
when he pops his head in to see if we're okay.
"Not much to ask, right?" I say.
He looks nonplussed.
"For God's sake, girls,
hasn't this all been sorted out?

I know Moira's been on to the head."
I snort.
"Well, if anything's changed, they're keeping it quiet."

Jack's so laid back he's horizontal, Mum complains.
"It's not proper parenting," she says,
"that pair ought to be more responsible,
your education matters more than messing about
with all these causes.
Cassie – sometimes I wonder
if that family's a bad influence."

REPRIMANDED

When I get home, Mum's in the kitchen cleaning up.
She stops when I walk in,
and sighs her complaints into the room.

"Cassie. We've had this conversation before,
you can't take the day off
whenever you feel like it,
even if you do think it's an important cause.
What did it achieve?

I had the school on the phone to me at work.
Mr Sheen mentioned some protest at the woods,
roadblocks? Vandalism?
That the police were called?
And you didn't answer your phone!
If university really is your plan,
you're going to have to behave yourself
and stop this messing about,
whatever you say,
it's   just   not   on.
Never mind the fees your grandparents are paying
for you to have a world-class education.
Why do you treat the chances you've been given
as if they mean nothing?"

Mum can't look at me while she tells me off,
she stares at anything but
my face.

"But, Mum, if I don't make a stand,
who will?
I can't just leave it,
stand back and watch
my future, the future of this planet, be destroyed –
I need to at least have a go."

"Not at the expense of your education
you don't."

Why doesn't she see
the importance of speaking up?
Mum didn't get to uni,
didn't get much further than A levels,
which she claims she failed,
and my brother,
well —
he's going nowhere now,
stuck here
doing nothing
at home.

APATHY

When Josh emerges out of his bedroom
the next day,
he takes over the lounge,
his feet on the furniture,
thin cheeks
patchy with stubble.

He lies down on the sofa,
looks at me, lights up,
farts and grins.
I have to get out, away from
Planet Josh: a world of magic mushrooms and
dope.

I slam the door
and am off.
Some of us have got things to do.

A REAL EDUCATION

The library hums with facts
and stories, other voices.
I inhale Mary Wollstonecraft's epic feminist manifesto –
the beginning is always today, she says.
She's so right: blind obedience is way out of date.

And then there's
Gloria Steinem
who called herself a
hopeaholic.

I like that word, say it aloud then write it down,
wonder if it would make a cool tattoo.

I read bell hooks,
who said
that what we **do**
is more important than what we *say*.

These women are fuel to my flames.
They remind me that
there is no excuse for giving up.

Appetite whetted with
ideas and inspiration,
I make lists and plan
action, change
at school,
at home:
the letters we will write
speeches I will make.

I think about our petition,
how we need to get those boys dealt with;
why should they get to swagger round school
with their mates
while their victims suffer alone?

I wonder if we could go on strike,
if every single girl in the school
could lie down
and refuse to move,
use their bodies to enforce a brave new world.

And if they think detention
or a couple of days' exclusion
are going to make me stop –
they're wrong.

I shop for something to eat on the way home.
I'll cook something nice to make Mum smile –
it's not her fault
she doesn't get it, I suppose.
But still, her passivity
needles me
like spikes underfoot,
as if I'm treading on barbed wire,
and I want to shout at her
to wake up to the fact that
she's not a doormat,
should not lie waiting for other people's feet
to trample her and
make her filthy
with their mess.

I tell myself I'm right,
tell myself if I keep trying then
someday I won't have to
fight.

Josh is asleep.
I stare at my brother's face,
mouth slack,
heavy breathing through his nose.
Are there any signs that maybe,
while I've been out,
he's changed? But he looks
blank   like he doesn't even dream.

Our house stinks again –
of cigarettes and weed,
his unwashed body and
unwashed clothes.

I hold my breath,
keep moving, although there isn't far to go –
the walls won't bend, expand,
he won't evaporate, or dissolve into bad air
that I can clear from the room
with an open window
or door.

Something in him doesn't understand
that being a man means more than just
your balls dropping,
facial hair sprouting,
acting like the world owes you something for nothing.

BROTHER

Mum cried when Josh left for uni, but I wanted to say,
Why?
He's a useless bugger.

Instead I patted her shoulder,
watched him disappear into the hall of residence
and crossed my fingers –

maybe now he'd wake up?

But not even six months passed before he came back,
his degree abandoned
thousands of pounds pissed up the wall.

MUM SAYS,

Don't be so hard on him.
It's hard for him.
He finds it tough — academic stuff,
and he's your flesh and blood.
Why not be friends?
You've only got one brother, you know,
you'll need him one day when I'm not around.
Come on, Cassie, make an effort — please.

I carry my frustration with me,
put it down on the counter,
slice it with the onions and garlic,
carrots, peppers and
sink them into the spitting oil.

It's late when Mum gets in.
She calls *Hello,*
and I hear her singing,
so I guess we're pretending
nothing's wrong.

We cook together.
She has forgotten to be disappointed or irate.
She tastes the pasta sauce I've made.

"It's delicious, love," Mum says,
and calls me 'Chef'.
She stands beside me,
stirring, fetching, carrying, then
yelling at Josh,
"It's on the pass!"

This evening he slumps into the room
and helps himself,
fills his plate,
taking more than his share,
then slopes off to eat in front of the TV,
making sure nothing is left over for tomorrow
so someone will have to shop and cook
and feed him,
and I regret the effort I made,
regret not spiking it
with something,

a rocket that might fire him out of his indifference.

He leaves his
dirty dishes for someone else to clean.
I wait for Mum to tell him
not to be a slob,
to demand he pulls his weight
that he earns his keep,

but she says nothing,
Gets up,
cleans up
after that lazy git.

I COULD SCREAM

But I don't.

I put down my fork,
clear away my plate
then walk into the living room
and say in a calm and reasonable voice,
"Look, don't you think
you could at least tidy up your own stuff?
Mum shouldn't have to run around after you
like you're a baby, Josh –
you're taking advantage of her:
she's not the hired help
and you're big enough and ugly enough
to look after yourself.
You'll be wanting her to wipe your bum next
or change your frigging nappy,

you great big baby.
Mum's been at work all day
and you've just sat in here
on your arse—"

Josh laughs at me, burps,
and says that he'll cook tea tomorrow.
"Come on, Cassie, chill out
why d'you have to be so uptight?"

I AM NOT A VIOLENT PERSON

by nature.
I prefer quiet.
The woods in autumn or spring –
soft with sun,
easy with rain.
But my feelings can come
like a raging storm.

And arguing with Josh
is like arguing with
a sheep.

He just bleats his laugh
and shakes his curls and
lights up another spliff.

I whack my brother, hard as I can.
He puts his hands up to his face,
cradles his nose, a drizzle of blood leaks towards his lip.
He's staring at me like I've gone mad.
"Cassie, what the hell?"

RELATIVE

He deserved that, didn't he?
Mum's yelling, "Get down here now
and apologize, Cassie."
But I can't.
I sit on my own in my room and cry.

Mum has the same shape mouth as me,
lips, a bow – naturally dark pink –
as if someone painted our faces while we slept.
But in no other way are we alike.

She has blue eyes,
and I have brown.

She is small, petite,
a flitting wisp of a woman.

I guess I must be
my father's child.

FATHER

is not a word
that gets used in our house.
Dad
or
Daddy
are equally banned.

But I reckon
he'd like the way I'm turning out.

IDENTITY

I wonder who I really am
and what it is I can become.

My phone bleeps.
I delete,
don't read,
don't want to see
whatever it is.
I'm not arsed what people say,
don't get bothered by stupid names –

Block, delete,
delete and **block,**
I shore myself up with
my own version of
who I want
to become.

Saved on my phone,
the last message Dad sent:
a photograph he took
that made front page news across the globe:

a schoolgirl
standing alone
in front of a mob, faceless and fierce in riot gear,

and she's reading aloud to them about
her right
to peacefully protest.

I stare at my stuff:
debate trophies, certificates for best results.
Ancient teddies and teetering piles of books.
There's too much crap
in here, too much junk.

I stand and look at my reflection
in the windowpane, in the dusk.

I message the girls. Tell them what I did,
made my brother's nose actually bleed,
argued with Mum, again,
and they comfort me.
it'll all be okay, Lori types.
Ria says: *just say sorry to Josh.*
Dilly tells me: *Cass, your mum's all right.*

AIR

I need to get out.
I sneak downstairs, out of the back door,
grab my bike and cycle away from home.

The roads are quiet, the woods deserted,
no protestors or police, just the barriers and notices:

No Entry
Construction Site
Danger
Keep Out

I sneak inside.

I know this route, the path
towards our spot,
like a vein that runs from my
heart to my hand.

Waiting in the dark, I settle into the earth,
stomach flat to the ground, lie still as stone.

And eventually
she emerges, alert, her head raised,
black and white stripes vivid on her face,
nose twitching, sniffing the air for danger.

We watch each other.
I don't flinch,
keeping so still, hoping she still trusts me,
that she remembers my visits, how I watched her
    cubs
tumble out of the set,

saw them roll and tussle in the long grass,
how I'm a friend.

I breathe the musty sharp
scent of the life here
and remind myself:
I must go on.

ATONEMENT

All week Mum's simmered with questions
that I haven't answered,
the *what's wrong with you?*
the *why are you like this?*
The *I would never have dared act the way you do.*

And I've said sorry a million times.

Saturday comes and we work in the garden.
Silently digging
in the drizzle
as Josh watches mournfully from inside.
We plant papery bulbs

that Mum stores from year to year,
dry and safe in the shed.
Our borders will be a burst of yellow come spring,
voluptuous tulips will lip their velvet way into the air,
glamorous and bold.

We dig all afternoon, and then
scrub the dirt from under our nails.
Mum hums like she's happy, a stupid tune
from kids' TV,
still stuck in the past
where the future is always beautiful.

The machinery
of my body is heavy,
clockwork heart and chiselled smile.
My true face
somewhere underground;
buried
a long time ago.

PART FOUR

NOW

ARMY ii

Monday morning,
end of September,
and
we're up
and at them,
on the move, slapping up posters on toilet walls,
in corridors
and on classroom doors.
PROTEST FOR THE WOODS!
HURT NOT THE TREES!
with the date of our next action
printed in vivid green.

In form Ms Lark asks me,
"So, Cassie, what's going on?"
and I tell her about it,
what we have planned.

Someone laughs.
I turn,
and see Henry,
he throws a ball against a wall

one of those small ones
that bounces hard
and ricochets
fast at me

a little bullet firing around the class.

Ms Lark frowns.
"Henry, please,
cut that out."
He winks at her, grins,
throws it again, once more, quite deliberate
and
fast.
I duck
before he pockets it and shrugs.

AGGRO

I'm in French when it happens,
puzzling over the subjunctive,
when there's an itch,
and I swat under the desk,

because it feels
as though
something

just twitched

its way into my space –
a fly, maybe, a foot,   a finger, perhaps.

The boy sitting next to me,
Simeon White, coughs.
Mostly we have a laugh mispronouncing words,
role-playing stupid situations
giggling over mispronunciations.
I thought he was a mate.
He shifts his chair a little closer
and I feel that itch again.

I look at Sim.

How can the hand that is crawling under the table
onto my thigh be his?
How can the fingers that grip my flesh, through my tights,
belong to him?

I push back from the desk, stand up
and swear,
"Get off me, Sim, you little shit."

There's laughter, someone whistles and applauds,
and Simeon's face is lava red –
he's about to stutter something –
but I'm sent out before he can begin
and only
        catch
                Henry's grin.

THEN

THINGS FELL APART

The night after we won the big debate,
I told Grandad I didn't want a lift and
Henry and I walked home from school
high on victory,
our route through the woods smeared with twilight,
orange and pink and red.

We talked and talked. Henry's voice
low, serious and confidential.

"Can I tell you something?" he said.
I nodded, listened, as
he painted pictures for me in the dusk
of a future,
confessing that he wanted to be a politician, even
the next prime minister,
"I'm not joking, this is for real, okay?"
and I said,
"Oh my God, Henry, yes!
You'd be so great, I mean, you've got the confidence
and well
whatever, you're so clever."

And I'll be your deputy or maybe Chief Prosecutor.
We'll change the world together."
I couldn't stop smiling
at the thought of this future.

But when he suddenly stopped walking
and turned, held me by my coat
and pulled me up close, and
his tongue
flapped in my mouth,
for a split second
I
froze.

Maybe my shove all those weeks ago
hadn't conveyed the message I thought it had.

But this was Henry
and he was my friend
and I liked him.

But not in that way.
Not at all.
I wasn't sure I liked anyone
enough to let them kiss me like that,
ever, actually.

The thought of it made me feel scared
and unsure,
as if I didn't quite fit in the world
where some girls were out to find exactly this:
a handsome, clever, popular boy.

"Um, no, sorry, Henry, don't," I said.
I pulled away, wiped my mouth and
Henry's face glowed red like the setting sun.
But whilst I was shaking
my head,
saying I wasn't into him
but that I was glad he was my friend,
he talked
over me, loudly, explaining
that he hadn't fancied me, at first,
but he couldn't ignore his feelings any more
and although I wasn't his type
he'd been thinking about me
quite a lot,
which was weird, right?
Come on, he'd been feeling the vibes,
he knew
that I liked him back.

I couldn't deny that

I'd been giving him the come on
all this time.

Getting angry,
he asked,
"Look, Cassie, do you want it or not?"

"No.
No, thank you.
I don't.
Sorry, but I just want to be mates.
Let's forget this, okay?
It doesn't matter, it's just a misunderstanding,
that's all. And if I made you think
that I liked you,
I never intended that, so,
I'm really sorry, Henry,
if it's my fault."

He still walked me home
        but it felt weird
        and no one was laughing
        any more
and when I tried to talk
        he
        shrugged and pretended
        he hadn't heard.

IGNORED

After that
Henry started blanking me at school
even though I didn't tell anyone what
had gone on.
I kept it quiet,
a horrible little secret
that spoiled everything for a while
and made my skin creep with disgust when I
   remembered
his mouth.
That slobbering tongue.

We avoided each other at lunch,
glared across classrooms,
he laughed if I got a question wrong.

And when I got tall in the next months, shooting up
beanpole thin,
he took the piss out of
my height
and flat chest,
and then
my hair
which he said was too red

and
my voice
which he said was too low,
maybe I was a bloke, he joked,
and my feet
too flat and big
flippers,
great big gobby giraffe-faced bitch.

WRESTLING

Arguments leaked into every lesson.
In science Henry said,
"Girls are weaker than boys.
It's a proven fact."

"Really?" I countered. "You sure about that?"

"Oh, yeah," he answered,
"not girls like you? Right?"

"What's that supposed to mean?" Dilly asked,
red-faced on my behalf.

"Nothing, just wouldn't be surprised
if Cassie was some sort of,
you know,
hermaphrodite."
He sniggered and shrugged and everyone joined in
whether they knew what that meant or not.

I turned to look at where he stood
behind his workbench
in the lab.
"And? So what if I am?
Why would that bother you, Hen?"

Dilly and I high-fived and laughed,
we
couldn't stop,
tears streaming down our cheeks,
a whole river of derision
that made him
angrier
than
any
of our
words ever had.

I could have gone for him then,

told the humiliating story of his kiss
and how he was rejected.
But channelling Lady Gaga was a much better diss.
Who the hell cares if I have a penis? she said
and I laughed even harder, remembering that.

LAUGHTER

is
artillery,
a bitter and beautiful fire.

It shells the enemy.
Rips them ragged with smiles.

NOW

BREAK

I'm loud with rage,
the fucking cheek
of Simeon touching me like that.

As I suspected, the reconciliation assembly
didn't quite do the trick
and
now they're trying to
prove that we can't stop them
getting away with this shit.

LUNCHTIME

I chair the student council meeting –
Dilly beside me
taking the minutes,
Lori marshalling lower school kids into the room.
Ms Lark is sitting cross-legged on the desk,
she smiles at me, taps her watch.

I wait for them to settle,
look out of the window,
watch the falling leaves –
orange, red, gold,
slipping through the sky –
I think of all there is to lose,
clear my throat,
wipe my eyes and smile
at the Year Seven who wants to start a collection:
a mini foodbank
to help kids in our town
without enough to eat this winter.
Hands wave in agreement as we vote to pass the
    motion.

If only it were that easy
to change the world.
Who says that?
Who whispers defeat into my ear?

"It *is* that easy to change the world,"
I tell the others,
and they nod.
Belief is in us;
against all odds we still have hope.

"It starts with a small voice,"
I say and point at Pierre
who's pink with happiness,
puffed up with possibilities,
"in a small room
in a small town
in a small country –
like a tiny seed planted
that becomes a forest,
the first drop of water
that becomes a well,
the first demand for justice
that grows into a swell,
an inexorable tide
of irresistible noise.
We are it, you guys.
If we stand together
we can change the world."

There are cheers,
and high fives,
but it's not time to go.

I'm going to say it. I have to.

"Unfortunately, we have a problem.

It's hardly news.
But I think you all know
of the sexism, the gross misogyny,
that's rife in our school."

Ms Lark looks up.
"What? Do we suddenly not want to speak the
    truth?"
I hold her eyes with mine and speak again,
"Ms Lark, it's facts.
There are boys who think it's fine
to harass the girls,
just this morning a guy touched me up
in class for a *laugh*.
The attitude to sex here
is frankly
disturbed."

Ms Lark coughs.
"Cassie—" she starts,
motioning at the Year Seven kids,
but I shrug and go on.
They need to know how bad it is.
They *already* know how bad it is.
So why shouldn't we say it aloud?

"We've got a culture here
where girls' feelings are a joke,
we're pixels on a phone,
a collection of holes,
barely human beings
in the eyes of some.
When the boys hurt us,
they don't even think once
about our pain."

No one moves.
I scrape a smile across my face
and sigh,
"So, come on,
I want to hear your ideas
about how to make a change."

There is a clearing of throats and someone says,
"It's not us that does that stuff,"
and the others agree –
it isn't them.

Mo shakes his head and looks pissed off,
arms folded, he stares at me, and says,
"We're not all like that."

"Mo, seriously, when did you last stand up for us?"
Dilly asks,
and he's about to answer when a Year Eleven girl, Eva,
    pipes up,
"Last week, a sixth-former grabbed my bum in the
    canteen
in front of Mr Sheen
and he literally said not one word.
In fact, he said I should wear a longer skirt.
You know, that's nothing compared to stuff they do
when we're not at school."

And just like that it begins.
I listen, can't tear my eyes away
from the face of a boy in Year Nine who says
someone told him
they were raped.
He starts to cry, says,
"I didn't know what to do.
What should I have said?"

Ms Lark is red-faced,
clapping her hands and asking for quiet.
"Okay, listen, don't talk over each other, please.
This is serious, folks,
these are safeguarding issues I have to report."

Dilly stands up.
I've no idea what she's planning,
but she looks serious,
and she has the floor, we're all watching and waiting.
When Cordelia Hall speaks, people know they should
    listen.

"Ms Lark, we need your help.
Because the girls of this school
and most of the boys
are not willing to collude
with a system
that enables the worst
to trample the best.
We want a meeting with the Head.
We want an opportunity to say
this has to end."

She nods.
"I hear you. Leave it with me.
In the meantime,
those of you who have shared
your stories this afternoon
will need to talk to the Senior Management Team.
Stay behind, please,
and don't worry.
You won't be in trouble for telling the truth."

Let's see what she does.
She's nice, decent enough,
but I don't think she has any clout.
I think we're going to have
to fix this ourselves.

Mum has told me to stay out of trouble
and I will try
for her
this term.

But I won't be quiet.

RABBLE ROUSER

We sit in silence
reading Jane Austen's *Pride and Prejudice*.
The words are a jumble.
I have questions I want to ask,
like:
why we need to know
about a book written several centuries ago.
Especially one about the manners and mores

of middle-class ladies
when there were literally people dying
in the mills and the factories.
How come they don't get a mention?
All these people care about is husbands
and haberdashery –

There are more pressing matters at hand.
I can't stop thinking about that boy
who's kept that secret –
a rape –
because he didn't know what to do or who would
    help.

It's like we've conspired in silence
for fear of raising a problem that can never be solved.

Misogyny has its own algebraic conjecture.
Prizes available for the first to discover
what makes
$M + F$
an unequal, unsolvable equation.

I look up from the page
and around the class,
ten heads bent in concentration:

what are they thinking?

The teacher catches my eye and holds it,
a challenge in her stare
to get back to work and
not to waste her time.

Well, what about mine?

I want to tell her that
the only waste
here is being perpetrated by her.
That, right now, there are students in this school
being interrogated
as if they are the problem,
and that whoever has touched or harassed these kids
is now
in their lesson, their free period, maybe the school
    canteen,
laughing with his mates.

I ball my hands into fists:
sometimes I feel like they're just killing time till we die.

But I think of my mum, and
nearly comply.

I CAN'T

"Cassandra, is there a problem?
Something you don't understand?"

"Nope." I slam down the book
and Mrs Joyce stares at me before she says,

"Then perhaps you'd like to share?"
She must know what's coming,
and is ready for it.
Maybe even relishing it,
the chance to school me in her thinking:
prove I'm just a woke idiot.

"Okay, yes, I would.
I want to know why we're doing this book,
given that its content
is completely irrelevant?"

I'm boiling up,
want to make something explode.

Mrs Joyce sighs and smiles and shakes her head.
"Cassandra, I thought you said you were a feminist?"

"Yes."

Someone groans.
Someone mutters,
Here we go,
she's off again,
someone else laughs
and someone says,
Shut up, Cassie, just get the work done.
I glare round the class,
Ria nudges my leg,
telling me she's there,
Ms Joyce goes on, carried away with her theme,
and so lost in her point
that she's missing what's right in front of her.

"A feminist would perhaps see
that behind the manners
and balls, behind the romance and soldiers,
there's an important socio-political point."

She waits.
Does she want me to provide the answer?
I don't.

But Mo does.
Oh Mo, betrayer of the cause,
you're clever

you'll get your grades without being teacher's pet.
Just because you're pissed off with me
doesn't mean you have to side with her.

My friend clears his throat,
"I think you'll find, Cassie,
that Austen's very concerned to explore
the plight of women – especially because
if marriage isn't achieved
society affords them no safety net,
unfortunately settling for Mr Collins
is the best for which Charlotte Lucas can hope –
would you rather see her starve on the street
or grovelling to her brothers for her bed and board?
Austen's pointing out
the injustice of this world
where girls
and women rely
on men
and the law has no interest in helping them.
I mean ... if you read *Emma* – you'll see ..."

Looks like he could go on and on
so I interrupt and say,
"All right, Mo – I get it – thanks,
you've got a point. And I know all that.

But I still think something a little more
radical and relevant might be good."

Ms Joyce nods, and holds my stare.
"How about we set up a book club?
Diverse texts?
Would that be a start?"

"I guess.
Maybe Mohammed could help?"

He nods, looks keen
and now I have something else to arrange.
I shut my book, gather my things and
without waiting for permission,
I leave the room.

GOOD DAY?

Not really.
Hearing my classmates, school friends,
kids as young as eleven,
describe being assaulted,

having some idiot feel me up
when I'm supposed to be studying,
isn't my idea of a good laugh,
but I tell Mum it was okay.

Mum's on her way out
as I get in and doesn't have time to talk,
off to work another shift.
I know she hates the evening hours,
watching it go dark outside
and waiting out the time
until she can come home and put her feet up and
watch a programme that makes her smile –
people baking or
faking fun – then
go to sleep.

At least it's not zero hours,
at least she has a job, she says,
that pays a good and regular wage.

She counts her blessings
as she watches the planes take off
through the dark windows of the concourse.
We don't mention the irony,
that she is grounded,

featherless, just skin and bone,
shoulder blades stark in her clothes.
She hasn't flown anywhere in years,
I don't even know where she'd want to go
if she could, and I wonder if she dreams of escaping
like I do,
                   I wonder if she'd like to leave me and all the
                                          trouble I cause
                                                behind.

"Get your brother something to eat, will you?
I made a stew –
you could heat it up?
Meat for him, veggie for you?"

I want to remind her
I'm not his maid,
and nor is she –
he has two arms and legs of his own,
he's fully grown –
and what the hell's she doing
making two lots of food?
He could have eaten vegetarian, too.
But I sigh and say, "Okay."

DINNER FOR TWO

I even set the table –
make it look like I'm making an effort,
like this is an apology for whacking him.
I turn up the heat under the pans
until they bubble,
I mash some spuds,
steam in my face,
taking out my frustration.

Cooking –
women's work,
until it turns into a matter of
professional chefs and then somehow,
suddenly,
they're all men.

But peeling, chopping, stirring,
rolling out meals day in, day out,
that's down to us –
cleaning windows, clothes,
dishes, floors –
all of that falls to me or Mum.
Has our biology designated us
more adept
at clearing up other people's mess?

Already I don't want to see him
when I call
that his dinner's ready.

I feel like throwing the plate of hot food
into his face,
but I don't.

I stare at the wall,
pick up my fork,
pretend to be civilized,
try to chew
and ignore the sound of him
shovelling forkfuls,
swallowing without tasting.
I could have served him up
a plate of mush,
he'd take it for granted
just as he takes Mum's wages
to pay for his phone, his clothes,
whatever stuff he buys,
the parcels that arrive, his cans,
his vape, his drugs.

Lumps of veg and mashed potato sit like
sodden cotton wool in my mouth.

"Nice day was it, Josh?"
I manage to say.
"Get out much?"

"Cool, thanks, Cassie,
yeah, it was pretty chill."
Provocative, I can't help myself.
"Smells like you didn't have time for a shower.
So, were you busy with something else?
Did you read the news?
Maybe apply for a job?"

He throws down his fork.
"What's your problem, Cassandra?"

I breathe,
pushing out a reply
that is even and unalarmed.

"Just making conversation."

I even manage to smile
but make the mistake of looking up
and into his eyes.
He doesn't blink,
shakes his head slowly.

"You think you're so clever, don't you?
You and your mates
doing whatever sad little thing it is
that makes you think
you're so much better
than everyone else.
Did you ever think that maybe not everyone's
as sorted as you?"

Am I supposed to feel sorry for him?
I put down my knife,
get up,
clear my stuff away
before I say something that
I will regret.

HABITS

I brush my teeth for a careful two minutes
with the toothpaste I like
that tastes so sharply and cleanly of mint
that it takes my breath away.

I wash my hair and rinse and rinse and rinse
until I'm so clean I squeak,
sit wrapped tight in a towel
whilst I listen to music, trying to find peace.
Wet drips land on my pillow.
I sit cross-legged,
and quiet in the refuge of headphones
that cancel out noise from outside, inside,
    wherever.

I like the ritual of candles, my room neat.
Everything put away in its place,
uniform hung up ready for the next day,
clean clothes in drawers,
books on shelves,
pens and papers on my desk in neat piles.

But I wish I could organize
something bigger
than my bedroom.

SATURDAY NIGHT

Heat leaps up from the floor
and into my hair,
sweats its way through my clothes
as drinks spill and I run from the bar
and back to the tables
with laden trays.

The night reeks
of beer and cigarette smoke drifting in from outside,
the rugby boys are in
celebrating a win
as the local drunks
sway their way towards oblivion.

Another shift while my friends party.
I'm working until we close
and have remind myself why I'm doing this,
why I'm putting up with
the boy in Year Thirteen who spews
tequila all over the table.

I fetch the mop,
wipe up.
No one apologizes

for the stink and the mess.
They don't even leave a tip.

"All right, Cassie? Give us a smile,"
some arsehole says.
I keep my face frozen and frosty,
pure resting bitch,
dodge sweaty hands, and breath.

My phone beeps and I
hide for a second round the corner,
read Dilly's text:
You coming, Cass?
Not yet.

Two more hours until I can join
my friends, and time taunts me, slows
as I imagine marshmallows melting,
Ria's guitar,
campfire spells.
Soft autumn night away from here.

HARRASSED

The things I want to say to them go like this:

Get your hands off
my arse
my waist
my back.

Don't move my body like that.
I am not an ornament,
compliant adornment to your
evening's entertainment.

Don't squeeze behind me,
just ask me to move.

Don't refer to me as eye-candy
or tell me to smile.

Don't fucking touch me again,
all right?

MIDNIGHT

I am not afraid of the dark,
not really, not so much
but   enough.

Knuckles keyed for battle,
I arm myself with household things,
tiny spears between my fingers,
teeth bared,
I walk and watch my shadow,
hope it sticks to me
undarkened.

The girls meet me on the corner –
safety in numbers –
warriors walking a world
that no one will promise us is safe,
where war is undisclosed and
hidden in sliding eyes,
the spittle of tongues that moisten teeth.

"How was Terry?" Dilly asks,
linking arms,
and I pull Lori to my other side
and she grabs Ria so we're all

connected, straddling the pavement,
 a chain, pure gold.
"Not so bad."
They're used to me moaning and the stories
of his roving hands are getting boring.

The girls are tipsy, silly with spirits
and I will have to drink fast to catch up,
we get to the woods and crawl
through the hole we've made in the fence.
I kick at it as I pass.
How can you buy trees?
How can you claim ownership of air?

ENOUGH

"We need a proper plan," I say
as we huddle by our tiny fire.
"Moira's got the next protest sorted,
that'll be great, but
this school thing.
It's stressing me out
that nothing's changed."

I'm drinking straight from the bottle –
sweet, sticky spirits dribbling down my chin.
Flames rise, drift, lick the darkness.

Mo shows up and Edward's here,
one of Henry's rugby friends;
Head Boy.
Someone has speakers,
music plays.

I watch Edward watching Lori and wonder
what he wants.

"Right, you lot, listen up."
I stand and wave them quiet.
"We're launching our petition
this weekend,
so get signing and sharing, okay?
It states that we want new rules in school.
Protection from verbal and physical assault,
the point is: we want to feel safe."

"And then what?" Mo questions, meeting my eye.

"Okay, well, we have more plans:
an assembly, stuff like that

but
if they ignore us, we'll walk out."

SUNDAY LUNCH

Grannie and Grandad serve nut roast.
Joshua looks at his plate and
makes a sound like he's throwing up.
"Don't be so rude," I say loudly, "how old are you?"
"Going to hit me again?" he asks.
Grannie shakes her head, tuts,
"Joshua, we're trying to eat less meat,
as Cassie says,
it's better for the environment and for our health."

My brother snorts.
"Know how many litres of water
it takes to grow one almond?" he taunts.
Grandad shakes his head.
"Enlighten us, Josh?"
"Dunno," my brother says, "but it's a lot."

Mum sighs, loudly.

"Bloody hell, you two, I give up.
Can't we just enjoy our food without a debate?"
Grannie smiles and turns to me.
"So, what's been happening this week, Cassie?
How's school?"

Mum chimes in again,
"Yes, what goes on in my daughter's world?
I'd love to know what she thinks she's up to now."

Joshua grunts,
says I'm hormonal
and need to take a chill pill,
give myself a break from being so woke.

I want to put my head in my plate.
Since when was Sunday dinner
all about roasting me?

Mum's off on a roll.
"No, hang on, I'd just like to know
how Cassie got to this point,
so full of opinions, like she always knows best.
I know – you were about twelve, or ten,
maybe earlier still:
probably when you were in the womb?"

Mum laughs at herself.
"You know, Cass,
you came out kicking and screaming,
red and angry and already outraged.
I think you've been like this your whole life
and it's not sensible, you know.
Better not to make yourself a target by being so loud."

"All right, Mum – yeah, thanks a lot,
could we maybe change the subject now?"

There's no point arguing,
I can't change how she thinks –
definitely not when she's had a drink
and reckons it's funny to take the piss out of me.

Grandad changes the subject,
talks about the woods,
how he's been in touch with the conservation people,
talked to the council,
written to our MP,
but that there's no chance of reversing the decision.
He's appalled –
but what more can he do?

HISTORY

It's a beautiful autumn afternoon
and Grandad suggests we walk off our lunch.
We scramble through the hole in the fence,
ramble through the trees to find the oldest oak,
the one we cannot stretch our arms around
even when we link.

Grandad says it's been here since time began,
this tree,
reminds us that buried giants lie
beneath our feet,
that wizards roamed the land
before we'd even dreamed of things
like cars and planes –
that this place is prehistory.

Josh listens, I watch his pale face flicker
with something
as we kick through the leaves
and he searches for mushrooms.
The sky is bronze and gold, yellow and red.
We pass lime trees, leylandii, holly, beech –
cedar, yew.
Grannie pats my arm, points out a nuthatch,

asks me if I've ever spotted a woodpecker, a cuckoo.

We breathe the still, warm air
as shadows dance and squirrels chase,
rabbits dart out of our way,
and the sun finds us somehow
in the peace.

PROGRESS

By Sunday night our petition's filling.

I send the link to Grandad and Grannie, and Mum.
Grannie messages back,
Well done!
Keep up the good work!
Then girls from our year, and the years below
begin to ping messages through –
thank you they say,
at last someone's doing something!
I type back that
it's the very least we deserve –
this is solidarity,

we are unity.
We can change the world.

And I delete the film,
sent anonymously
before it can play,
of a girl
in a dark room
on her own

stretched out

on a bed.

OCTOBER

MONDAY AGAIN

In every room
new invisible lines separate
Us

        and

                Them.

At breaktime
antipathy pops and crackles like wet wood, drifting
   smoke
of suspicion, making it hard to know
who's a friend.
The girls gather round.
We take up space
in the common room,
as much as we can,
even if we're outnumbered
three to one.

I speak first,

"Right, listen up.
Petition's doing amazing, so
next steps:

we see March – show her what we've got –
and tell her we want the assembly as well.
That should make it real,
we'll share the true impact
and educate that lot in the reality
of what it's really like to be girls in this school."

I elbow Lori, she nods,
opens her phone and
shows us the messages,
sent after the petition went live.

Which anonymous coward?
Jamie again?

Whores.
Fuck your petition.

We read text after text of
warnings,
slurs.

The language is explicit,
vicious,
all about attack.

Threatening my friend
with
rape.

I snatch the phone and hold it under Edward's nose.
He reads, then
passes the phone to Mo,
who passes it to Luke.

"Report them," Edward says.
I shake my head.
"What? And get the blame, get slut-shamed?
My phone confiscated?
Nope, don't think so."
I stand up and tell my friends, the room,
"You know what? This stops. Right now."

ACTION

I leap over bags and chairs and tables,
no idea what I'm going to say,
landing in their territory.

"Oooh, Cassie, what's up?"
Henry drawls from where he's sprawled,
but I know he knows.

Jamie sniggers,
"Cassandra, babes.
You know what you can do with your petition?
Sit on it,
and on my face."

Henry laughs,
as Jamie goes on,
"You know what you need to calm down?
One of these,"
he grabs his crotch, grinning,
"a really big,
really hard
one in your mouth,
maybe then you'd shut
        the fuck
                up."

WHAT?

I want to slap back,
but I can't,
tongue flat and
useless,
inarticulate.

CAVALRY

"Jamie, you arsehole," Dilly screams,
"how dare you? What the fuck?"
She's exploding,
shouting, her finger pointing,
while Lori's on the table,
radioactive with rage;
my friends are a dervish of sound,
a cacophony of defence
and all while some dickhead's filming
the whole hideous thing,
they're still just
        laughing
                at me.

Camilla's watching from Henry's side, silent,
mouth open,
drowning,
tangled in the thick of their mess –
tied up in his knots,
because it's all about the banter,
                    babe,

                                        isn't it?

HEAD BOY

Ed steps in front of me, a human shield,
and in the deadliest of voices announces,
"James, come on. That's too much.
Apologize to Cassie right now."

"Ed, mate, I think you'll find I won't,'
Jamie says, turning his back on us.

Ed's in Upper Sixth, so smart and so serious,
Lori says he's one of the ones,
who honestly means it
when he says

he's proud to call himself a feminist.
But he's still their friend.
Sod this.
I don't need him.

"Ed, I'll sort it." I push forwards,
finding my feet and my voice.
I lunge for James,
to strangle him with the chain he wears round his neck,
but Dilly and Maria,
hold me back.

The girls don't want another fight.
A repetition of the night it went too far,
last party of the summer,
when I made some boy's nose bleed.
After that, I swore I'd keep calm,
tone it down, smooth my sharp edges,
sand the rough textures of my words and thoughts.
Give these fools the benefit of the doubt.
But, God, it's hard.

Dilly explained afterwards that he'd been serious,
the guy with the pitch-black hair and long thin hands,
who played the guitar and sang songs about the
    darkness

inside us all.
She said he liked me.
I said, "Big deal."

"Apologize," Ed repeats,
"Cassie's well within her rights
to report this to the Head,
and we're all witnesses, right?
Seriously, James, you could be expelled.
You simply cannot speak
to Cassandra, or anyone, like that."

"Oh, fuck off, Edward."
Henry stands up,
even bigger than Ed.
"Why can't the silly bitch just take a joke?"
Jamie laughs again, and begins to mince
around the room, jumping up on chairs,
pretending to cry, rubbing his fists to his cheeks.
"Who's going to make me apologize? You, Ed?"

He laughs, spitting crumbs
and licking salt from his lips,
then crumples the packet of crisps in his fist
and drops it on the floor,
like a gauntlet thrown.
But Edward doesn't flinch.

"Quite possibly, James, yes."
He clears his throat and straightens his tie.
Six foot of him, brick shithouse build,
prop forward,
not inclined to make trouble, nor to look for a fight,
but ready to take my side,
and Mo's light on his feet, he shoves Henry
in the chest, squaring up,
Luke's right behind him
and it begins to feel
as though the entire common room
might pile on.
Girls cluster close,
there is anger everywhere, sharp words, hot breath,
boiling frustration.
      spitting and hissing,
           bubbling up and over, splashing the air.

And then the bell rings.

I don't get my apology
but

I will.

SHHHHH

Henry wants me quiet,
or at least
a cooing thing,
sweet little birdy,
tamed and caged.

He hates the sound of my squawk;
says he'd like to see me stuffed,
take a needle and stitch my lips tightly shut
or simply break my beak with his right hook.

He'd prefer it if my mouth
were merely a receptacle;
he'd love it if I would only
parrot his opinions.
But mostly he'd like
to wrap his meaty hand
around my neck
and silence me for good.

But I'm going to scream
until someone hears,
turn myself into a wailing
siren,
insisting

that
this is an

emergency.

Silence isn't golden, as they say,
silence is
a sea of drowning
girls.

DON'T TOUCH

"Are you all right?" Edward asks.
I shrug his hand off my back.
"Yes, I'm fine.
I'm going to see Dr March.
She was on our side once.
I'm reporting this.
He can't threaten me like that."

"I'll come with you," he says, and the girls nod.

Dr March ushers us in and we stand

side by side.
She's poker faced, doesn't invite us to sit.

"What's happened? I have two minutes;
if we can make this snappy, I'd appreciate it."

"I've been threatened.
It's Jamie Jenkins. Henry Riordan.
People have evidence, videos.
They're behaving like animals.
We've started a petition, and they don't like it,
so they're trying to intimidate us into silence."

Waiting for her to speak
is   like waiting   for a firing squad.

Dr March looks from me, to Ed, back to me and sighs.
She leans forward, giving the tiniest sign
that she cares.
"I appreciate that you want to make a change
but, and I mean this in the best possible way,
I think we need to let this die down.
Stop fanning the flames.
This petition of yours,"
she sighs again,
"could well create more problems

than it will solve.
And let's face it, Cassie, you're not renowned
for your tact.
Perhaps be a little less quick to react."

She can't be serious.
I step forward.
"Dr March. Please, listen.
It's not just the petition.
We want to hold an assembly
and explain our aims.
Education's the way ahead. Right?
Please, give us a chance to make everyone understand."

"I think
there are some members
of our school
who may not feel that
        education
is honestly your goal.
They might think they're being singled out,
that this is some kind of   witch hunt,"
(I snort, she frowns)
"a deliberate attempt
to undermine their sense of self.
We cannot afford to look

as if we are adopting a misandric approach."

"That's not our intention at all," I snap.
She must know that she's talking shit.
"We want to give everyone the tools to deal with
any sort of abuse.
And actually, that includes the boys.
Some of them have been hurt, too, but
do you think they can talk about it?
No."

"I'm sorry, Cassandra.
The teaching faculty will decide
how to move forward from here.
Our investigation has commenced
and Mr Sheen is taking the lead.
I understand your passion, and I admire
your desire to speak up, and do what's right,
but perhaps pour that passion into your studies
and attending your lessons,
which you are currently missing,"
she looks at the clock,
"and leave this matter with us."

She's already on her feet
ushering us out.

"No way, Dr March.
We're going to fight –
we won't give up,
I mean – it's worth it, right?
For the future?
I mean – do you even read the news?
Women dying, all the time, victims of male violence,
girls as young as twelve, abused. Younger still.
This is serious stuff that you can't just dismiss
as wokeism, or whatever they say it is.
Women are being murdered
by men
just for walking home.
Only three per cent of rape prosecutions end in
    conviction –
four fifths of women have experienced sexual
    harassment.
No wonder girls won't come forward –
they're too ashamed and
too afraid of being blamed and branded as a liar or a slag.
Dr March,
you've got to face facts."

"Excuse me?"

"Come on. Help us. Please."

SHE'LL THINK ABOUT IT

Ed shrugs.
"That's good," he says.
"Well done, Cass, you made your point."

"Did I though?"
But he's already gone,
leaving me standing outside her office,
alone.

FAIR PLAY

At lunchtime I go off site
to sit by myself
for a while, try to process
what happened
and why
it made me
feel so   vile.

Why can't we speak out without fear?
It takes courage to say

I survive, I persist,
and I get it,
no one wants to be seen as the victim
and we don't want pity,
we want action.

I sit in a nest of moss.
Breathe,
in
and
out,
slow – like they say helps,
I try to clear my thoughts of all the
mess.

The noise flies through the trees,
a sonic boom
that jolts me
out of peace.
I walk back towards the playing fields,
stand disguised on the edge of the woods,
safe in shadows,
and watch the end of the match.

I watch Henry run, barrelling fast and huge,
the ball under his arm,

his legs thick pistons of power,
shoulders braced.

He dives the ball down.
It's done and they pelt
back towards school.
Henry leads,
head thrown back
and Ed, beside him, arm around him,
in celebration of
victory.

PRIVILEGE

Dr March agreed
Lori and Edward and I will be allowed to present –
a diverse team, making the point
that this really isn't about pitting girls against boys.
We can work together, as equals and friends.
We can remind everyone that she was right all those
    years ago.

We meet in the library on Friday after school

to organize our pitch.
Lori takes out her stack of cue cards,
impossibly neat handwriting filling the space,
painstaking work, designed to persuade
everyone of the truth.

"Can you believe March agreed?" I ask.
"Maybe she's actually on our side in this."

"Maybe," Lori says, "I hope so, Cass."
She takes a deep breath.
"But listen,
before we go any further
I have something to say.
I want you to know that
when we present
I'm going to talk about just how much worse
it is to be dealing with all this
as a black student."

I look at my friend,
my beautiful, brave, bold friend,
feel my skin begin to heat,
I nod, and take her hand.
"Shit, Lori," I say, "I'm sorry.
I didn't mean to

leave that out.
God, I should have said.
That's definitely got to be part of it."

"I know. You didn't mean it
but when you tell me about bell hooks or whatever,
it's kind of
ridiculous, you know,
like you're preaching to the converted?
And when you don't mention how half the abuse
    I get
is so obviously because I'm black.
I dunno, Cassie –
it'd just be nice to feel like my friends got that."

I clear my throat and nod.
She has a point.
A massive one.
I'm a dick.
Self-centred, egotistical fool.
Other people have problems
bigger than mine.

I hug my friend.
Thank her for her support and ask her to
forgive me

my ignorance, my blindness, my one track-mindedness.

Edward has looked down at his notes as we've talked
but when he looks up,
he and Lori smile at each other
as if he already knew what she'd planned, and
when he brings out his stack of cards
that match hers
and smile that smile they have –
a secret between them –
I nearly say,
Good, right, you two go ahead.
You do it. Take charge.

I nearly get up and go,
run outside into the rain, down the road
to the woods and the trees and the place where
there is silence.
No more voices,
no more messages,
no more pressure.
No more expectations.

Maybe I just want to
be allowed
to

disappear.

"Cassie, are you okay?"
Edward snaps me back
into their friendship
as he touches my arm.
"Yeah, I'm fine." I grasp for normal,
something upbeat to change the tone.
"Look, I know, in the assembly why don't we
put on a bit of a show?"
Edward creases his brow,
and waits for me to explain.

"So – what if us two, me and Lori,
dress up, I dunno – like a stereotype,
fifties housewives, our hair in nets, wearing aprons,
full on red lipstick, wielding wooden spoons –
and walk into the hall to a soundtrack of
maybe,
a bit of Beyoncé?
And then, when we get to the stage,
we'll whip off our costumes
and do a big reveal –
superhero outfits, you know,
capes and stuff.
I thought it might be cool?"

Edward looks puzzled.

"We don't want to look as if we're just *shrews*,

maybe showing our sense of humour could work."

"But won't that trivialize our message at this stage?"

I sit back, fold my arms and Lori nods.

"No, Cassie's right.

It'll make them sit up.

Listen. Get involved.

We'll still keep to the facts

and how this impacts *all* of us."

The premise of our presentation will be

the damage done

by division.

The pain caused by the pornification

of our society.

That it isn't good enough just to say

you're an ally,

you need to act.

That our school must be a safe haven from

all the shit

that's flung in girls' faces

from the second they're born, held up by the heels and

designated weak.

We want to say feminism isn't just for the few,
it's for every person on this planet,
every woman,
natal or not,
who's felt belittled in a world built
for men.

"And not just white women either,"
Lori says, reminding me again.
"I want to talk about how it is for girls of colour,
how race matters in this,
that white women, that goddamn white school, needs
    reminding
that feminism isn't all about them."

CLEVER BOYS

know how to talk themselves out of trouble.

Word gets round,
and the week before our assembly's happening
we huddle at lunch wondering what
they have planned.

Camilla, who talks to us more and more these days
in little gasps, when Henry's not looking,
leans over.
"He's been to see Dr March
and she's agreed it's only fair
to allow the boys to talk, too.
Otherwise, Henry said, it was biased.
And she agreed!"

Ed grabs Lori's hand,
pulling her back into her seat before she
darts over there and starts a fire.
"Look, it's fine.
What can he say that we can't refute?
He's all right, you know, Henry,
a lot of it's just hot air."

I like Edward, but he's naïve.
Why can't he see
that now we are going to have to argue over
whether misogyny actually exists?

"I guess Dr March has to be seen to be even-handed,"
Edward says, oblivious,
as he spoons up soup,
"but I agree. It's probably not appropriate."

Camilla rolls her eyes.
"Didn't you know?
Jamie's dad basically funds this school.
Those new labs last year?
All his doing.
March has got to give them what they want.
Basic economics, folks."
Camilla looks me in the eye, shuffles closer along the
    bench.
"Sorry, you know, about before,
at the start of term
when I acted like you were being unfair.
I know what they're like."
We meet eyes, hold a glance,
I nod, and ask,
"Did something happen
with you and Henry, then?
Did you split up?"

She shrugs.
I don't ask anything else.

THIS IS WHAT I'M GOOD AT

right?
Using my words.

Last year I stood up in front of the school
and told them all why
I should be Student Council Chair.
People voted for me.
There's proof of it.

I have won debate after debate.
I know how to express myself.

So why don't I want to do this today?

ASSEMBLY

It's the day before we break up for half term,
first thing,
everyone's half asleep
and dreaming of doing nothing next week.
Lori and I stride down the central aisle,

in our costumes,
Beyoncé bold,
every time she sings "*Girls*"
we wave our props –
mop, spoon, cleaning cloth.

We dance
through hundreds of our peers
assembled to the left and right,
who look up, stare, begin to wake up.

My skin stings with adrenalin
as the music plays
and the talking starts,
as our friends cheer and whoop,
and we swagger and strut,
quick twerk before the teachers can tell us to quit –
and then the big reveal –
superheroes.
We're here for it.

"This is our feminism," I begin, climbing up on stage,
taking the mic, calming them down,
"we're here to re-educate you
on the meaning of that word.
It's not up for debate that women are equal –

this is the twenty-first century, right?
No, what you need to understand is
that we're here for every person who has been
made to feel small,
treated like
they don't matter at school.
We want you to know that we won't be
harassed any more.
And we want to explain:
our petition is for good.
For change."

A chant of "feminazi" begins at the back of the hall.
"Get your tits out," some idiot yells.

I stop.
My throat closing up,
stomach liquid, hot.
I wait for the teachers
to find the source and shut them up.
But Sheeny's pretending he can't hear it,
reading a newspaper by the looks of it,
and Dr March doesn't even seem to be listening.
She frowns at them, waves at me to hurry things up,
even looks at her watch.

I have to style this out
and go off script.
I raise an eyebrow and sigh –
point a finger at my head.
"Brains are the new breasts, folks,"
I patiently explain.
       I get a bit of a laugh
                    and stride
                         centre stage,
                              praying my legs won't give way.

But they're all looking at me.
And all I can hear is the laughter,
all I can feel is the eyes
and the pressure
of
coming up with answers.

I clear my throat,
cough
and blurt out,
"We've had enough.
It's time to accept that
No
is actually a full sentence."

But no one's listening now, I've lost them,
they're talking and shifting in their seats,
bored by me.
I fix my eyes on Dilly's face,
she's mouthing,
go on,
but I can't.

Not when it's so obvious no one cares what I say.

Lori leaps up,
takes the microphone from my hand.

"Hey, be quiet, you lot, come on,
Cassie's right.
Our generation has been sold an abhorrent lie.
We've been told we're equal,
but if the events of the past months
have told us anything
it is this:
we are not free.

Speaking as one of the girls of colour in this school,
did any of you ever stop to think how this impacts our
    community?
Well, I can tell you right now.

It's worse.
The way men look at black bodies, brown bodies
isn't right.
For every bra strap you've had pinged,
times that by ten.
For every dick pic –
God, I have folders of the things,
I've saved them on my phone –
Dr March, if you're listening, I'm happy to share.
With the average age of exposure to porn
being eleven years old,
it's no wonder our generation sees girls
in those terms.
With the attitudes to colonization and patriarchy
so embedded they're as powerful as gravity,
it's no wonder you think that strangling
us in bed
will turn you on –
that hurting us is, somehow, hot.
So sign up right now
and show the school that you want to see something
    done."

Henry's lot boo,
but others clap and cheer
and Lori punches the air, sits down,

squeezes my hand
and smiles at me.

EDWARD

The hall quietens, strains forward
to catch his every word,
and he's the best of them,
I can see that,
and I can see how Lori looks at him –
if I have to share her with a boy,
it might as well be him.

Ed speaks slowly, serious and intense.
"We cannot deny, as much as we'd like to,
that we live in a world that is unjust.
But our school can be a place where we challenge that,
where we sign up to be better boys and men."

God, they're actually listening.
Not one whimper of dissent.
If this were a popularity contest
I know who'd win.

Ed goes on,
"In a world that hears male voices
and accommodates us
we need to show we see it's unjust.
We all have mothers, sisters
aunties, cousins, friends who are girls –
but you shouldn't need reminding of that,
it shouldn't be the only thing that spurs
 you on to treat your fellow students
with the humanity they deserve.
We insist that from now on
sexist language or
behaviour
or attitudes will not be ignored."

He looks out at them, the rows of lads
who outnumber the girls and
steps to the edge of the stage,
meeting eyes,
holding stares.

"We must agree that
Castle College will not tolerate
discrimination of any kind.
We must demand new school rules
that enshrine the rights of every person to study here

without harassment.
We must demand that there will be appropriate
    punishment
for anyone who abuses another student
with actions or words."

He sits to thunderous applause.
Edward smiles and we join hands
although I want to scream

that it's not fair,
no one cared when I spoke,
no one listened,
I was just whining,
being woke.

But Edward's voice –
how much power it has.
When exactly are my words going to matter as much?

UNITY

I shove the thoughts aside.
We are friends,

two girls and a boy
sharing the stage.
If only it were that easy
to change the world.

Maybe it is that easy to change the world.

But now it's Henry's turn.

COCK(Y)

He's crowing like a strutting rooster,
riding the wave of the bellowing cheer
that accompanies him up on to the stage.
I can see the man he'll be, and almost already is,
it's in the confidence of his stance
and the heavy certainty of his voice.
A proto prime minister, of course.
Support swells as he shoulders his opinions into the
    hall.

"Let me begin, my friends, by stating,
just so we're clear, how much I love the

fairer sex, dare I say it, our better halves –
our Castle College girls."

There are whoops and he points to Camilla and winks
as she cringes in her seat, folding herself up small.
"I'm a ladies' man, right?
I'm happy to own it.
No shame here."

There's laughter, and he smiles, holds a hand up for quiet.

"But what I won't tolerate, folks,
is the demonization of the male.
So – I'm wielding my freedom of speech, right now,
to try to counteract some of the *nonsense* – ahem –
I mean *arguments* that have just been raised.
No one is denying the importance of women
to the human race.
How could we?
Women keep children alive."

More laughter, a chorus of agreement.
Edward clears his throat beside me.
I look at him,
he shrugs
and half smiles.

"But let's just remember that without men,
women would lead primitive lives.
I warn you —
do not underestimate a man's value in this world."
He thumps his chest.

There's another cheer from his crew,
who Dr March glares at until they shut up,
while Henry smiles, holds out a hand
as if to say,
Hang on,
I'm not done.

"Historically, women have been spared the worst work."
He shows us pictures,
flipping through a slide show of
Thors, muscles bulging,
then soldiers and builders, grunting,
lifting, heaving, preening.
Henry tells us that Amazonian warrior
women are a myth,
that we are biologically weak,
that our demands for equality are so far removed
from fact as to be an absolute
nonsense.
"Is there a female equivalent of Sisyphus?

Of Hercules? Of Atlas?"
he demands, and provides his answer:
"No, there is not.
Women quite simply do not share our strength."

The teachers stand, ready to quell more roars of
    support,
but the hall echoes only shocked silence.
Henry has them in the palm of his hand

and he turns to me, takes a step closer,
says right into my face,
"I'm sorry, Cassandra, that you feel quite so bitter.
I mean, cheer up, love – you should be celebrating the
    fact
that it's illegal now to pay a woman a compliment.
Pretty soon there'll be gender apartheid –
we won't even come near you,
well – you'd probably like that,
given your, ahem, preferences –
so why can't you be content?
Women have never been so damn free.
Give all this whinging a rest, stop ovary-acting,"
he winks, thinks that's so witty, so clever,
"and embrace the privileges of your sex.
Cassie, sweetie, relax,

and allow yourself to be comfortably oppressed,
as you were for centuries until this silly feminism
reared its ugly head.
Isn't it time you admitted you love to be dominated?
As the great man Nietzsche said,
You go to women? Do not forget the whip.
Basically, babe:
know   your   place."

UPROAR

Henry smiles at me,
without a flicker of remorse,
the superpower of shamelessness
needs no props, no further words.

I speak, though no one hears, the hall's so loud,
with students arguing and calling out,
and teachers bellowing for quiet.
I say,
"Henry, misogyny kills.
Yet according to you, misandry
is somehow worse."

He shrugs, it's just us, the conversation now
as intimate as the days when we'd plan
our dreams, share private jokes.

I force myself on.
"Seriously, Henry,
why do you hate me?
Why don't you want to help?"

It's too late.
He's turned our assembly into a joke.

A row of sixth form girls
                    stand up,
                    walk out
as the Deputy Head hoots at them above the
    crowd.
"Pathetic,"
Mr Sheen hollers,
"grow a backbone, girls!"

Dr March strides through the mayhem
onto the stage, white-faced, grimacing
as she struggles to silence the riot,
the chaos of jeers,
the fists pumping the air,

the howls that Henry is a neanderthal
who should be expelled.

Henry leans back in his chair,
doffs an imaginary cap.

Through gritted teeth, the Headteacher speaks.
"Right, I think you've all had your moment.
Indeed you've entertained us this morning,"
she turns to look at me,
"but feminism, Cassandra,
is more than costumes and gimmicks
and frankly, Henry, your ignorance is astounding.
I'll speak to you both later.
The rest of you –
back to class.
It's time to get on with some real work."

The bell rings
The hall empties
And I sit there. An idiot.

FOOL

I take off my superwoman head band,
pull on my blazer,
thank Edward and walk away.

We weave through the corridors
that echo with the sound of laughter.

My knees shake
and it's only Lori's arm
        holding me up
as the words of Henry's speech
                reverberate around the school.

SUMMONED

This time it's both of us,
Henry and I,
standing in front of the Headteacher's desk.

"What a disgrace," she says, shaking her head,
"you should both be ashamed.
Well? What do you have to say?"

She looks at Henry.
"You know, young man,
some of the things you said today
were deeply concerning.
I can only presume that was some sort of joke?"

He grins and runs his hand through his hair,
shoves his hands in his pockets, sticks out his chest.
"Of course! It was just a laugh, a bit of fun.
I respect Cassandra,
one hundred per cent."

I roll my eyes, don't argue. What's the point?

"Good," March says, still unsmiling,
looking at me as if she's expecting objections,
then nodding at my silence
misreading compliance.
"I look forward to an apology from you both
for those appalling scenes
and hope you understand
that this matter is now
closed."

PART FIVE

NOW

HALF TERM

First Saturday of the holidays shows up,
cold and cloudy,
and I drag myself downstairs,
weights hanging from my fingertips.
I haven't slept.

Mum's sipping tea, like normal,
offers to make me porridge, a hot drink.
"You're up early, love.
Are you going somewhere?
It's not Moira's wretched protest is it?
In this weather?
Don't you think you'd be better off
leaving them to it?
Staying at home and having a rest?
You look worn out."

"Nope."
I'm not going to stop.
And if she doesn't get that
then she doesn't get me.

"Mum—"
I begin, but she's already over by the sink,
washing up, so she doesn't hear me speak
over the sound of the taps running, the sink filling,
the kettle boiling, again, the endless cups of tea
that solve nothing.
"Listen . . ."
I mouth my words into the steam
and she hears
precisely
nothing.

And then my friends are on the doorstep, waiting.
"Josh, go with your sister," Mum says,
shaking her head,
"and make sure she's okay."
He rolls his eyes but comes slouching behind,
grabbing Mum's toast on his way out and
we're off again.

"You okay?" Dilly says.
I nod. Fake smile.
Don't mention the disaster yesterday.
"Course, look, this is brilliant."
Protestors from all over the north
are converging in town.

Streams of them stopping traffic,
marching down the main road towards the woods.
And we have painted ourselves with our message:
DON'T TOUCH
it's written on skin, under our clothes.
Time to make them really take notice.

I'm the first to pull off my coat
and my hoody
and my top,
skin goosing with cold
as we freeze in the wind,
in our underwear, right at the front of the crowd.

"Bloody hell, Cassie," Josh says,
"now I don't know where to look.
Put your bloody clothes back on."
But it makes the press stop
and photograph us.

I'm in the middle of the shot,
mouth wide
and screaming.
How much more desperate do we need to get?

CAMILLA

We weren't expecting her
but she's here
with a smile that asks for something:
acceptance, I think.
We smile back at her as she slides into our line and
helps to swell the blockade on the edge of the wood.

"You were so good in the debate, Cassie,
what you and Lori said –
it made so much sense."

"Don't lie," I tell her,
"it was a disaster.
I was totally humiliated."

"No. Honestly. You were great." She swallows,
shivers, rubs her neck, shakes her head.
"I thought I liked Henry, thought
that he was cute."

I want to ask what happened between them,
don't know if I should,
if the question,
"Camilla, did he hurt you?"
is too much.

She laughs a laugh that sounds like pain.
"He's treated me like shit.
I don't want to say any more, not here.
But I reckon you can guess?"
I nod.

"You know, Cass, well, you probably already guessed –
Henry's got it in for you.
It scared me, the stuff he said.
It was disgusting, I told him to stop,
but he just laughed again, like it was a joke.
I just wanted to say, you should be careful,
watch your back."

She touches my arm
and there's real kindness there.
I believe
that she's good and
isn't taking the piss,
that Henry isn't using her
to get at me.

"Is that your brother?"
she asks, giving me space, stepping back,
and we look over to Josh, who
looks more alive than I've seen him in years,

talking and nodding furiously,
then speaking just as loud and fast again,
gesturing back at the trees,
stabbing his finger towards the town,
his blond curls caught by the wind,
cheeks pink with cold.

He turns, grins, waves, jogs over.
"Okay, Cassie – so listen, right,
these guys over there, they're
going to set up camp.
I'm going to join them, tell Mum?"

"What do you mean?"
I laugh, he has to be joking.

"I'm going to do it –
like you always said –
actions speak louder than words?
So we're going to set up in the trees.
Proper Swampy and everything.
They won't be able to shift us.
Won't be able to cut anything down,
not while we're there.
What do you think?"

IDIOT

Mum stares at me
when I tell her what Josh has planned
and then back at the picture
of me on the Facebook page of the local rag.
"Cassie, did you really have to?
You're half naked.
I thought you said you were emancipated?
And what do you mean, your brother's gone to live
in the woods?
Have you both lost your minds?"

"I am emancipated.
My body is mine
to do with exactly as I like.
I'm in charge of it – not you, or them.
And if I want to use it
as a way of getting some attention
for a cause,
if I want to take my top off,
then I can."

"Attention?
The attention this will get you
is precisely the kind of attention you need to avoid."

RECLUSE

Although my body might be present
during my shifts at the bar,
when I'm eating dinner with Mum,
when I'm with my friends and
we're riding our bikes
into the freedom of air,
(no bells or lessons or Henry or James
for now)
my mind drifts
to the questions
and the truth
and the silence
and the proof

that nothing has changed.
I lost.
And I'm on my own.

OCCUPY

Josh messages me and asks
for treats:

crisps and beer and clean clothes.

I carry his stuff down to the woods
and we meet in a patch of sunlight
beneath the big oak.

"Thanks, sis."
He hugs me. It's weird,
but nice. Better than fighting
over pointless stuff.
I lean into his side
although he smells
pretty bad.
"What's going on?" Josh says.
"You okay?"

No,
I want to say,
I'm not, I'm really so not,
but I can't.

I can't tell my brother
that I'm a loser
and I want to give up.

HOLIDAYS

Grandad calls up and asks
if I fancy a day trip somewhere fun.

I say thanks, but no, I have stuff on.

I stare at pages.
Don't read.
Sit in the bath until the water runs cold.

I turn off my phone.
Don't know what more I can do.

NOVEMBER

HERE WE GO AGAIN

Is everyone looking at me?
Sniggering behind their hands?

Dilly hugs me, it's as if she knows,
and whispers that it's going to be okay.
"Cass, the petition has done so well,
we have so many names,
March will have to care."

I smile and nod,
play along, then I have to go.

First day back, I'm meeting Ed,
can't let him down,
or any of them,
especially my friends.

I walk along the long white corridor
towards the Head's office.
The walls are heavy with cases
bearing trophies –
evidence that Castle College boys are

the fastest the biggest the boldest the bravest
and I'm lost inside their
triumph, feel it closing in,
stealing the air,
reminding me not to
presume I matter
one bit.
I jump when I hear a yell,
"Hey, Cassandra."

I turn.
Yup, it's Henry,
Camilla pinned by his side.
Why's she with him?
I thought they'd finished?
She looks wooden,
a puppet, strings gathered
into a fist.

Henry's already too close
and laughter curls at the edges of his mouth
as Camilla tries to pull him away.
"Hen, come on."

"Shut up," he says,
then looks at me.

"Fun the other week, wasn't it?
I enjoyed that –
teaching you a nice little lesson
about your *feminism*."

He smiles and shrugs, his face tanned
from his half term on the slopes.
"We could take our debate further, if you like,
I reckon you still have a lot to learn
like, who the fuck do you think you are, right?"

When I turn my face away
he grabs my arm.

"Henry, come on," Camilla tells him,
"leave it, please,
leave Cassie alone."

"Is there something you want?" I spit, finally
speaking up.

Henry sneers.
"Want?
Nope not really, not from you,
I reckon I've had enough,
            but,"

he leans in again,
                    still gripping my arm,
"you know, your mate Dilly's hot."

He grins, so clever, so close.
"Tell Dilly I said
she's definitely my type."

Camilla looks as if she's about to be sick.
Ed's striding towards us.
"All right, mate?" he says, greeting his friend.
"Yeah, good, man, thanks."
They slap backs, share grins.

"Come on, Cass, we're late—"

And I'm walking away, by Edward's side,
glad he can't feel
my pulse racing
or see my legs shake.

DEMANDS

Dr March's face falls.
"Let's keep this short and sweet, shall we, folks?"
But when Edward hands her the petition,
over one thousand signatures demanding change,
she places it face down on her desk.

"Thank you. If that's all,
the bell will go in a moment.
Get to registration, please."

"Dr March?" I say.
"Don't you want to know what it is?"

"I think I can guess – it's your petition, yes?
I thought we were drawing a line under this?"

Edward points at the pile of paper.
"Could we ask, Dr March,
what action you plan to take?"

She answers, although a grimace
twists her face in pain.
"The school will conduct an investigation –
as I've said before, this isn't an issue

with which the student body should be concerned."

I throw up my hands. Finding my voice.

"We *are* the student body."
I gesture at my feet, my legs,
my chest, my head,
       step towards her, showing myself,
       and the light from the window is in my face
       as if I am on stage
       under a spotlight, taking my cue
       to speak, and soliloquize.
       "This is it, right here —
       we're not an abstract thing,
       but real-life human beings.
       Dr March, come on,
       can't you see?
       This matters so much!
       We need your support!
       Please!"

"Cassandra, enough."

"No, I don't get why
you can't see that
pupils in this school don't   feel   safe."

"How absurd.
Listen to me.
Staff have your best interests at heart.
And students who have been named
are being dealt with.
I can assure you of that."

Are they?
Not that I've heard.
And I want to say to this woman:
Actions Speak Louder Than Words.

GENTLEMAN

How can Edward be so patient and polite?
"It's just how I am, I suppose,
I don't enjoy conflict
and I think more is achieved by working together
than forcing people apart.
March is okay, Cassie,
you just have to keep on her right side."

"Ed! Don't be so bloody diplomatic!
That won't get us anywhere.

Aren't you angry?"
He grins and shrugs.

"Of course I am.
And I love your fire.
I think that together, you know,
you, me and Lori,
we're kind of a formidable team.
And I'm pretty certain we're going to win."

ARE YOU OKAY?

I don't go to my lesson,
I hide in the library, right at the back,
huge stacks of encyclopaedias and dictionaries
a perfect disguise.
I take out my phone and send message after message.
But Camilla doesn't answer.

I send another at break, just in case, and try to
catch her eye across the common room.

I'm here for you, Camilla

I repeat
hope you're okay?

But she doesn't even glance
my way.

MATHS

That afternoon, last period,
we are nine, not twelve.
No sign of
Jamie, Alexander, Miles.

Lori catches my eye.
We speak without words,
wondering if it's evidence
that March is taking action,
and I wonder whether or not
Henry will still be sitting pretty
in the common room tomorrow,
presiding over his coterie of hate,
or if he'll have vanished, too.

Maybe Camilla will have spoken out
and done
the thing I've been trying so hard to do.

REACTION

Tuesday morning,
I walk into the form room and
Henry's standing on a chair,
yelling for quiet.
He sees me.
Catches my eye.

I can sense it,
more trouble.
Right here. Right now.

"It's a bloody witch hunt," he declaims,
pointing my way,
then looking at the crowd of sixth formers
who've gathered to watch.
"It's outrageous, an absolute joke.
My dad's coming in,

he'll tell her we won't let this go.
He'll get his lawyers and put the shits up
March with her wokey crap.
We'll show her who's in charge round here, right,
    lads?"

There's another bellow of support.
He grins,
the smile of a crocodile,
all teeth and tongue and lips.

BARRAGE

We can't block and delete fast enough.
The sickening salvo
of abuse
makes me want to throw my phone
into the toilet and flush.

"You know this is illegal," Edward says,
"I hope you're keeping evidence.
I really think you should be reporting this."
He's looking over my shoulder

at the stuff I've been sent
in just the hour since
Henry announced his campaign.

"We've complained
over and over again.
They say they'll look into it,
but they must be blind
because apparently
there's nothing to see.
Time for
shit to get real,
I guess."

By afternoon school
Jamie's back
and laughing in my face
in maths.

I can't take it.
I stand up
and walk out.

AFTER SCHOOL

I walk to my form room.
Ms Lark is sitting alone at her desk
marking a stack of papers,
and she smiles when she sees me,
hovering by the door.

"Cassie," she says,
"how are things?"
I shrug.
"I signed your petition.
You know, it's young people like you
who give me hope –
no one will ever shut you up!"

I slump onto a chair, look down at the floor,
want to say that actually
I wish my childhood didn't have to be a war.

"What's wrong?" the teacher asks.

"Our petition didn't work, did it?
It didn't make any difference.
What's changed?"

Ms Lark can't look me in the eye.
"You're doing well, Cassie, please,
remember that.
The Head's in a difficult position
and although it might not seem like it,
she's doing her best.
I know there have been a huge number of parental
    complaints."

"But it isn't enough.
It feels like no matter what we do,
no one gives a damn."

"They do, they are, and they will.
But you need to give it time,
change won't happen overnight."

I can't believe the way she's talking,
she sounds like my mum.
"Ms Lark! No!
Time's running out!
And their time's up."

She holds up her hand
as if to stop the storm of words
but

my mouth runs on, leaving the rest of me behind
and
beforeicancensormyselfitallcomesout

"It was me. All right?
I'm the one who wrote that post.
      The first one.
         I was hurt, attacked.
         That was my story everyone saw online."

I stop.
Open-mouthed.
Oh, God,
what have I done?

Ms Lark stares.
"Sorry, Cassie, what did you say?"

No.
I stand up
I'm out of here.

It wasn't me, that girl.
I won't let it
be me.
I am not her.

No.
No way.

But the memory, the truth of it,
is acid in my throat and mouth,
and the heavy bands of shame
that have kept me silent all this time
are around my neck
my wrists
my waist.

Maybe
I have to break
to be whole again.

"It was me,"
I repeat, speaking into the wall.
"Last summer,
         me who was
                  assaulted.
                        I was raped."

WHAT NOW?

I turn and watch her trying to find the words.
Can't bear the silence.

I should just leave.

Maybe she can't help.
But that's her job, isn't it?
To make this go away?
Maybe it's too late.

"Wait, Cassie, did you report this?"
 the teacher says at last.
"Have you told anyone else?
Your mum? Your friends?"

I shake my head. Hover by the door.
I will never tell my mother what happened to me.

She walks over,
takes my hand.

"Please, come back, sit down.
Can you give me the details?"
Can you tell me again what happened?
Let me try to help?"

"No. I can't remember much,
I think maybe my drink was spiked.
But it was Camilla's party
and my whole year was there,
someone has to know who it was.
What are we going to do, Ms Lark?
What am I supposed to do now?"

HOSTAGE

I remember all of it,
from the beginning,

the little boy who wanted to play
a game that demanded
I take off my pants,

too small and bewildered to understand
the undressing, or touching, or what I was supposed
   to do
when he put his   penis

in my hand.

Another day,
still nursery school age,
the boy who pissed on me,
too impatient to wait his turn
for the toilet
but instead opened the door and aimed
and fired
all over my lap.

Then the bigger boys in the park who liked games
that involved holding girls
flat on the grass
and kissing them until they couldn't breathe,
the boys who pinned girls in cupboards
whilst their friends stood guard.
Where did they learn that any of this was okay?

AND NOW?

Ms Lark moves her marking aside,
and asks quiet questions,
makes notes,
nodding, careful, her voice gentle and low.

We finish.
She tells me I have to leave it with her,
makes no other comment, no judgement.

"What are you going to do?
Are you going to tell my mum?"
I ball my fists
and she touches my hand
briefly, smiles in sympathy, I think.
"Cassie, you know I have to pass this on
to the safeguarding lead.
And after that I'm not sure how things will proceed
but we will do our best to help you deal with this.
I'm sorry this happened to you.
I'm sorry you've had to go through this
on your own."

"Who's that? Safeguarding whoever?"

"The Deputy Head."

I'm twisting my school jumper,
so tight round my finger,
my skin bloodless, whitening.
I think of him, Old Sheeny, knowing   this
about   me

and start to cry.
I don't want him to know.
Don't want him to sneer and mock and say it was
all   my   own   fault.
"And what will he do?
Will he tell the police?"

"Yes. And your mum.
Cassie, you need their help.
And any time you need me,
I'll be here."

But she doesn't say
that this will end it,
sort it,
or that she can make everything
okay.

RAPE

What they did to me is
a word I'm trying to erase
but which keeps on growing,

even though it's small –
just four letters,
and like other
expletives,
it has teeth
and fists
and tears chunks from me,
holds them, hanging bloody from its lips.

I go to the bathroom,
lock myself in a stall.
Ram my fist into the wall.

AT HOME

Alone, curtains closed, lights off,
I shut my eyes tight and try not to think
of the night
last year.

They'll say
I was
stupid to have been out so late,

stupid to have been at the party,
stupid to have been drinking

so much.

But what they did to me
was not my fault.

THEN

THAT NIGHT

We'd finished our exams
and after months of being trapped indoors
we were out
and freedom felt
brand new.

It felt like we were owed something,
that the world had secrets it had been withholding.
We wanted it all
and swallowed fast furious shots,
tottered in unfamiliar heels
to parties
where we roamed,
masked by alcohol,
almost unrecognizable.

Camilla's party was the biggest of all
and Dilly was too hot,
she wanted to swim in Camilla's pool and cool off.
Lori agreed. Ria and I shrugged and went along.
We staggered up the drive that twinkled
with lights and rattled with cans,

clinked with bottles,
smoke curled and heat rose
and I remember thinking it was
hell, so hot and crowded and loud.
Bodies pressed together
in and under the water,
on sofas, in corners –
you could taste the hormones,
and I wanted to leave, retreat
to the woods and breathe in fresh air
away from the madness
that this freedom had unleashed.

Someone offered me a glass of something
and I took it,
drank,
not tasting
just hoping I'd relax,
stop feeling so
awkward and strange.

Camilla staggered towards me in a gold bikini,
weaving her way through masses of people,
she hugged me, slurred into my hair,
"Yay! I'm so glad you came, babe!"

I drank some more,
sat on the side of the pool and
dipped my feet in the water.

Someone dragged me in and under –
sick in my mouth,
I pulled myself up,
gasping for breath,
coughing water and vomit out of my lungs.

It didn't sober me up.
I was cold and wet
and wanted to go home.

Someone gave me another drink and I stood,
shivering, sipping,
watching things spin, feeling my legs
begin
to give.

Inside, I put my back to the wall, and inched upstairs,
looking for quiet.
Camilla's room was dark and cool.
I collapsed on her bed,
I lay back,
wanted to curl up
on her crisp cold sheets and sleep.

NOW

YOU DO NOT REMEMBER

the fact of not breathing
that isn't a fact
but a panic.
The arms that rope you.
The fact that your mouth opens to scream

                                    then beg
but no one hears.
And then there is only drowning
in fear.

Their laughter.
                    Your choking silence.
Their entitled fingers.
                      Your body breaking.

You cannot make anyone feel the scorched air, that
heat,
they cannot smell the singeing of skin, tiny hairs, pores,
   scars
and your fear.

Like an animal –
trophy hunted.

And beyond the walls of the house, the moon sits in
   the sky,
moving counter-clockwise,
showing the same face,
seeing nothing.

HERE I AM

I can't stay in bed, waiting for sleep that
eludes me, as evasive as
peace.

Rain drums on the window
and outside the wind shrieks and throws
violent gusts.

I get up, creep out,
wishing I could leave my thoughts behind
like a pile of clothes
thrown to the floor
by the bed.

But that night will follow me for ever, now.

I wear it,
the memory,
dark red and heavy,
it scratches my skin,
too tight at the neck, too long at the arms and legs,
so I can't run
or speak.

No one stirs or notices me disappearing
as I cycle, buffeted and blown like
trash, down empty streets

to the trees.

LOSS AFTER LOSS

A mound in the middle of the road.
A sole streetlamp illuminates the scene
in judders and twitches of light that is caught by the
    gusts
that snatch
my breath.

I throw my bike to the ground
and walk towards the hump of body
that
is still warm.
Last breath barely drawn
but gone, nevertheless.

I can smell the petrol,
see the spill of oil
and know what happened here.

Hit and run.

I pull this beautiful creature
into my arms.
My funny snuffling friend,
her eyes now blank in
her black and white face.
She is heavy with death.

I can hear the pain of the trees,
the ache
as the tears of the world fall,
watching me walk,
laden with this
burden.
It is beyond words.

We sit
in the rain,
under branches that reach skeletal hands
in prayer to skies that are dark with loss,
weeping for everything
we have destroyed.

GET ME OUT OF HERE

"I'm not going back," I tell my mum,
"it's just not happening,
I don't give a shit what you say."

"Cassie, don't swear at me."
Mum is shaking her head,
deaf and blind to my pain.

"I'm sorry. I am. But seriously.
It's too much.
Dr March just doesn't give a toss.
She's ignored all our complaints –
did you ever get a reply to that email you sent?
I'm going to leave whether you like it or not."

I run upstairs, lock myself in my room
and pace
acres of silence.

HEADACHE

There's nowhere to be alone,
the woods are full of bodies, noise, protestors,
and I have to leave it, leave them to fight
that fight without me for now.

I bury my face into my bed
and scream into the mattress.

I shut my eyes,
and lie in the dark,
trying to will away the pain in my head
and my heart.
There are no tablets in the cabinet,
guess Mum's taken the lot,
or Josh.
He came home for an hour today, coughing,
looking thin.

He smelled bad, even worse than before.
But he was smiling,
and looked happier
than he has ever been.

I shake.

It's stress,
I tell myself –
diagnosis:
I have too many men to
castrate –
metaphorically,
or maybe not.

I grip the bed,
try to stop the sway and swell,
the gasping fear, that I'm drowning here, alone.

Who made me superwoman?
Avenger of the weak?
Oh yeah –
I guess that idiot was me.

Tears come in torrents and I slap my face –
because when did crying ever help?

I pick up my phone
and squint at the stories
on the website
that updates every day,
screaming with new testimony.

I've been looking for hours.
Maybe that's why I'm seasick with pain.

There are hundreds of Henrys,
so entitled and shameless.

Not all men are bad,
I whisper, the cliché no comfort.

FEARLESS

Fear less.
Easier as an imperative
than an adjective.

There's too much to be afraid of.
Stop – think about it

for a moment

                or, don't.

Better not to know,
maybe
better to be
naïve
than understand all the ways
fear can deceive.

My mum is afraid of everything
and I get it,
can feel the ghosts on my back
at night,
the presence of eyes
that scrutinize
and see
only weakness,
that wait to find
a way to undermine.

Fear less
or
fear more –
and protect yourself.

PERFECT TIMING

I'm lying on my bed wondering what's next,
maybe I'll just join Josh in the woods,
when Mum calls upstairs,
"Cassie, have you seen this?"

She shows me the letter from the Head:
a school inspection.
Okay.
Maybe this changes things.
It's a chance.
But it means we'll need to organize fast.

It needs to be timed carefully:
maximum impact,
maximum exposure of the truth.

The girls come over and
we send message after message,
sitting on the floor in my room
which is now mission control.

Our call to arms reads:
Hey!
Listen up —
all you girls

and all you boys,
every single ally to our cause –
if you support
JUSTICE and
EQUALITY and
the RIGHTS of EVERYBODY
to learn unharassed, and unintimidated
then you are cordially invited
to join our strike action.

The message spreads
like a wildfire
let loose
on dry ground,
it hits, and grows
so many shares and reposts
that the air glimmers with our smiles.

Lori whoops, dances around the room,
Ria leaps off the bed.
I try to share their confidence and laugh a little,
smile at Dilly who's watching me with narrowed eyes.
Mum yells at us to stop making a racket,
that the ceiling will fall in,
as I tell them all
this is it:
our time has come.

STRIKE

Women of the world have been striking for years,
decades of brave feminists
have said
time's up,
screw this,
me too,
give us our rights
or you get no more of us.

So.

There will be no more work.
No more dutiful prefects
being dutifully perfect,
no more cooperation
with school examinations
or school anything –

There will only be mayhem
until we are heard.

PART SIX

STRIKING BACK

"Shit, it's cold," Dilly says
when we meet at six thirty a.m.
outside the school gates.

We swore we'd be the first,
ready to greet the inspectors with a nice little dose
of truth.
We stamp our feet and wrap our scarves
a little higher and tighter,
pull down hats, pull on gloves,
zip up thick coats.
She links my arm and we huddle close,
warming each other
in the frozen dawn.

"Look at the sun," I say,
"it's coming up, Dills,
it's a sign, don't you think?"

"Every dawn brings new beginnings," Dilly smiles,
"and this one will be epic.
They'll be here, soon, the others,
and we're going to make so much noise
that they'll have to listen.

We've been polite, Cassie,
we've waited, we've been so bloody good
and cooperative.
But now it's time for something they won't forget.
Just remember, I'm here beside you,
always, okay?"
Edward's next.
He has a flask of coffee, camping mugs,
silver foil parcels of toast,
and is tall and handsome in a thick woollen overcoat.
His brown eyes smile at me.
"Ready?"

"For anything," I tell him.

PICKET LINE

By 7.30 a.m, the line stretches and curves
                          around the wrought iron gates
from the teachers' car park,
                          to the student entrance,
a blockade of bodies,
                          and the wall of our voices grows
thicker and stronger.

We form a barricade,
        no one's getting in
                and no one's getting
                        out.

We hold our banners high
as teachers drive up
and some students try to sneak inside:

DO NOT TOUCH!
HANDS OFF!
WE DESERVE TO BE SAFE!

I lead the battle cry
as more students arrive
and we demand they do not cross our line.

NO IDEA

I don't think even Henry was anticipating this.
He steps towards me,
flanked by his friends.

I let a sneer curl my lips
as I take in his
designer suit
and shiny leather shoes that creak
and crunch on the ice.
I spot Jamie.
"How nice to see you," fake smile.
"Daddy make another fat donation?

Henry shakes his head.
"What kind of absurdity is this?
Get out of our way."

The girls close in at my sides
and his boys do the same,
falling into formation,
ready to ruck.

Dr March interrupts.
She hates it, hates us, hates me,
hates the fact we're on TV,
hates the thought of being humiliated
by a girl of seventeen.

She stands on the steps with a megaphone,

like the ones they use at sports day,
yelling to be heard,
but our chanting grows,
the boom and holler filling the sky.

The inspectors stand beside their cars
watching, arms crossed;
one of them already has his clipboard out
and is taking notes.

March descends, still talking,
tightly belted in her coat,
and wends her way

               towards where I stand
               at the front of the line,
               in front of the local TV anchor.
               "So, girls,
               what's inspired this anger,
               why are you striking?"
"Haven't you heard?
This school won't listen to its students.
We want change.
But Dr March isn't interested in what we have to say."

               "Tell me more, please, explain."

I'm about to tell her exactly what's provoked
this strike,
that no one gives a damn if students here are safe,
when March steps between us, palm in my face.
"Cassandra.
You need to call this off.
This is no way to achieve your aims."

"What is, then?" I ask,
"what are we supposed to do
to get your attention?
More humiliating assemblies?
More pretence and empty promises?"

Dr March shakes her head.
"Can't you see how much it matters?"
I'm on her level today,
standing tall
and refusing to shrink
into the acquiescence she'd prefer.
March speaks through tight lips.
"You think they're here because they care?
They're just enjoying causing havoc,
playing at being adults
who think they know and understand
how the world works.

What you don't seem to realize
is that you're wasting precious time –
your education,
that thing you seem to take for granted,
is the very thing that will set you free."

I draw a breath,
keeping calm,
and the sun glows
in the white sky
and my friends sparkle, pins of light.
"So what you're saying is
because we're young,
anything we say doesn't count?
That what has happened to us is, what?
An accident?"

"Yes, Cassandra.
I am aware
that the world can be
difficult
and unfair.
And I know you believe in this cause,
but most of those joining you
have no idea
what it is

they're fighting for
and you have no idea
what it is you stand to lose."

SCAB

The teachers begin
      weaving through the students
and for all I tell them
      to hold the line,
          the threats,
and promises whispered,
      the calls to parents
and suspensions mooted
      are enough to
send them
      trickling
          back
              inside.

I swallow my screams of
traitor
and watch them abandon our plan.

But stage two is up my sleeve
and I nod,
give a sign to the girls
who pass the word along the lines
and we file inside.

READY

It's English and we're finally finishing
Pride and Prejudice.
A tapping of fingers on tables,
a jiggling of knees,
restless eyes flicker and flit.
But nobody speaks when Ms Joyce asks
what we think of the multiple
marriages at the end of the book.

The inspector sitting in the corner
leans forward,
Joyce raises an eyebrow
but still nobody says a word.

I mean,
there's a lot I want to say

on the topic
of marriage as a form of social control,
how houses were built to contain women,
keep them behind locked doors,
constrained and monitored
like battery hens,
but we're not cooperating.
No one utters a syllable,
not even Mo
who gives me the faintest of nods when I catch his
   eye.

We're on countdown now,
sixty seconds until we
stand up
and
walk out.

I'm holding my breath
when, out of embarrassment,
a girl at the front pipes up,
ruining the moment,
breaking the pact
with some old rubbish
about unity and stability and comedic closure,
and before old Joycey can tell her what a star she is,

that's it —
I I a.m —
it's time to act again.

STEADY

I push back my chair,
push myself to my feet,
look round
as the others rise.

Yes, here we go, thank God,
they're still on my side.

"Cassandra? What's this?" the teacher says.
"Excuse me, can you sit back down, please?
The bell hasn't rung.
I will dismiss you when it does."

I don't answer Mrs Joyce,
ignore her protest
as she has ignored mine,
and we walk as one

to the door,
open it
and
file
out
and

GO.

I march down the corridor,
leap down the stairs,
praying that this will work,
that I won't be
a lone body –
I need them
to care.

But from every corner of the school
footsteps ring,
the thunder of feet,
more than I'd imagined
would join in.

Adult voices demand,
"Get back in the classroom.
Please, return to your seats."
But no one is listening
and they can do nothing
but fall silent, watching us
leave the building.

We're an army,
a presence,
a storm.
We are a force to be reckoned with,
a great tide of girls
and boys
on the move.

I begin the chant,

CHANGE WILL COME
CHANGE WILL COME
CHANGE WILL COME

and it's an anthem,
a chorus of rage
and pain,
of determination and hope,

as we stand outside in the wintry cold
in our blazers and school ties,
from the smallest Year Seven,
shivering and brave,
to Edward,
Head Boy,
and when I give the cue
we lie down on the frozen ground
and refuse to move.

PUBLICITY

Cameras snap.
Lori's dad's contact at *The Times*
is grinning at this scoop,
the prestigious private school
where the kids are refusing
to acquiesce to the edicts
of the management team.

I reach out, grab Dilly's hand   and Lori's on the
                                                             other side,

    then Maria, Camilla and Ed, Mo   link and pass
                         it on,   a chain of determination,

bodies looped   and locked in resolution.
I turn my head and look at my best friend
and she squeezes my fingers, whispers,
"Just look,   Cassie.   You did this."

I don't think that's true,
it was all of us.

At least two thirds of the school
is horizontal,
a sea of insurrection,
a rising wave of voices and determination.

We will not be moved,
not until
someone promises to
make the change
we deserve.

DISPERSE

Teachers, school inspectors, traitors
observe from the side lines
and Ms Lark steps between us,

negotiating arms and legs and heads
until she
finds me
at the centre.
"Cassie, Dr March would like to see you now,
and Edward, too.
Can you come with me, please?"

Her cheeks are pink in the cold
and her eyes are pleading.
"Come on, Cassie, just come and have a word."
I sigh, sit up, ask,
"Why? What does she want?"

"To talk about resolving the situation.
This can't go on."

"I've given her plenty of chances to care.
You too.
What's different now?
Is it because these inspectors are here?"

"Cassie, come on."
Ed's getting up. "Let's go,
this could be good news,
let's see what she wants."

I know what she wants.
She wants me to tell them
to go back to lessons,
she doesn't want a school
dead of hypothermia.
She doesn't want to be sued
or in the news,
or seen to be losing control.

"Cassandra," Dr March says,
as I stand before her,
"this is absurd."

"Actually, I think it's pretty cool."

"Cassandra. I'll say it again: enough is enough.
Please tell me this is the end of it?"

March strides out onto the tennis courts
and speaks through her megaphone.
"Get back to lessons, immediately,
parents are being contacted
and any further disorder
will not be tolerated."

SNOW

Shivering Year Sevens
and trembling Year Eights,
frightened by the Headteacher's threats,
look at me, waiting for my help,
but I can't protect them, can only tell them
that I reckon if we stick together, we'll be okay.

I look up at the sky
which is heavy and low
and watch
the first snowflake fall.
I put out my hand
and catch it as
hundreds of eyes wait for me to speak.
I don't want to be the one who gets them in trouble –
but I can't back down.

"It's okay," I say,
"You know, if you stay out here,
they won't be able to punish you.
If we all stand firm,
united, as one, they can't expel us all.
We will make our point.

Honestly – look what we've already achieved.
You've all been amazing!
We're making a change."

They mutter, shift and sigh.
Eyes plead and voices question.
"How long do we have to say here, Cassie?"
a girl in Year Eight asks, her plaits dotted with snow,
and I shrug,
and want to say:
as long as we can,
for ever
if that's what it takes.
"Look at us!
They say we're snowflakes,
but we don't melt!
We are snow-blossom,
beautiful, strong.
We have proved just how powerful
we are,
together we're an avalanche."

"Come on," Lori calls, joining me,
"don't give up!" and there's a cheer, we settle back
onto the cold, wet ground,
last ten minutes more,

then another fifteen
and Ria begins to sing,
her voice a bird
soaring above the bodies,
and Lori joins her,
they sing that we're queens, rebel girls, rebel boys,
that the revolution is coming,
that we're dangerous,
should be feared,
have righteousness on our side.
I grip Dilly's hand,
meet Lori's eyes –
> we share the fear
> that it can't last
> and the hope that it will,
> and it does,
> shoulder to shoulder we lie.

FROZEN

The little ones are turning blue,
chattering teeth,
and frozen lips
whimpering with the cold.

We get to our feet
and walk the rows,
whispering thanks,
telling them to go
and defrost inside.

HEADLINE NEWS

I go to find my brother,
away from my mother
who is incandescent, then tearful
and demanding I'm remorseful and apologize to
the Headteacher.

I climb through the broken fences and locate the
    camp,
call up into the tree where he's perched
like some bedraggled bird.

He clambers down,
sucks on his vape then hugs me.
I show him my phone and hand him a flask of hot tea
and he scans the article, tells me that he's proud.

"Look at this,
front page of the frigging *Times*,
they're calling you the new Mary Wollstonecraft,
Joan of Arc,
nice one, sis, you're making waves.
Has Dad seen this?"

"No clue. But don't read below the line.
They say all kinds of evil stuff.
Not sure what my next move is
to be honest, Josh.
I guess we'll have to see what March does."

I empty my bag,
give him the packet of biscuits
and flask of soup, some fruit, and he grins
and we sit on a fallen trunk as he eats.

"You starving or what?"

"Yup. But it's cool."

"How long are you going to stay out here then?"

I stare up at the sky
and the barren branches,

I wish I could climb up there

                    and wait for spring.

"As long as it takes.
I'm actually doing something for a change
and this lot are decent, you know,
Cassie – you should join us,
it's good, away from all the other stuff.
Clear your head, get sorted.
Sod that lot."

"Maybe I will," I tell him.
It'd be easier than being at home.

SUMMONED

School is beginning to smell of Christmas.
A huge tree dominates the atrium
but I don't feel like celebrating.

Nothing's been forgotten
and March has kept me waiting all week,
the sword of Damocles dangling on its thread,

her face grim with foreboding
in assembly this morning.
As if I care.

It's dark outside and everyone's gone home
or is tucked up safe and warm in the boarding house.

Mum, and Grandad and I sit in silence
in an empty corridor, waiting.

Dr March is sitting at her desk
and doesn't stand up
when her secretary ushers us in.
She looks at my mother.
My grandfather.
Finally, at me,
then frowns and speaks,
"Cassandra's time here
at Castle College is up."
I'd been expecting it, but my stomach
swoops.

"She's been given chance after chance
and has made no response
to any disciplinary measure,
I've tried to be fair

and hear her out,
but now I have to take this step –
she's disrupting the education
of everyone else."

They look at me.
I shrug.
All right,
whatever.
I guess
I'm done.

"Hang on a minute," Grandad says,
"are you telling me that Cassandra has lost her place
because she stood up for her beliefs?
Surely, that's exactly the kind of young person
this world needs?"

Dr March shakes her head
and swallows before she replies.
"Mr James,
your granddaughter is rude and disruptive.
Her principles, her ideas, are sound
but the way she goes about enforcing her views
is fundamentally flawed."

"I don't agree.
You know, there are journalists still calling the house –
I'm sure they'll be very interested to hear about this."

"Is that a threat, Mr James?
Because I won't be intimidated."

Grandad leads us out.

"It's a promise, Dr March,
that you haven't heard the last from me."

We file down the corridor,
through the grounds,
to the car park, where in the dusk,
I see Ms Lark filling her boot
with boxes, files and bags of books.

Looks like she's leaving too.

She lifts her hand, opens her mouth as if to call to me
and something makes me go over.
"I'm sorry," she says,
"Cassie, I tried.
I reported everything,
I spoke to Mr Sheen, followed up three times.
He told me he had things in hand.

I don't know what went wrong.
But I've resigned.
I don't know if that's right, if it'll help,
but I wanted to at least try
to make a stand."

IT CAN'T END HERE

Another long and lonely day.
I sit on my bed and think about this
war with no aim
except for absolute elimination.

I need an atom bomb or
a lightning bolt –
an obliging act of God.

It's half past one,
my friends will be sitting together at lunch,
and I'm here on my own.

I sit on my hands to stop the shaking,
to stop myself from reading the messages –
daily missives

that remind me
no one is missing me.
My phone buzzes,
my hands twitch.
I hold in tears,
grind my teeth.

And I read the message —
of course I do.

gutted you're not around, Cassandra,
but anytime you fancy another big hard dick,
let me know.
it was hot last time,
we enjoyed it
— me and the boys —
especially since you were too drunk to talk,
you know, you're so much nicer when you're quiet.
maybe there's a little life tip there, Cassie,
as I've said before,
why not shut the fuck up?

It's anonymous of course,
some burner phone, the cowardly git,
so he can't be traced, and reported,
so he can try to avoid all consequences
but I think I know exactly who this is.

PART SEVEN

DECEMBER

CONGRATULATIONS

The message in my inbox
brings the first smile to my face
in what feels like
months.

Dad.

Well done! he writes,
You're making waves!
Saw your wonderful face made front page news.
Couldn't be prouder of you, Cassandra —
my teller of truths.

RESOLVE

If you've turned yourself up as loud as you can,
screamed your throat sore,
yelled yourself hoarse
and still no one has heard,
then what comes next?
Is silence the inevitable consequence?

You could
run away, I suppose,
try to find utopia in a different world.

Or you could
                    try

                            and try
again.

I don't give up,
it's not my style.

We've been patient,
tried to fight our battle
politely,

asked you to respond,
but all you've done is react

so maybe
we're going to have to get really nasty.

I need to be the bullet in my own gun,
the blade of my knife,
the army of myself.

LAST CHANCE

My room feels small
when the girls cram in after school.
The air is dry
and my throat tight with plans.

Lori puts on a film,
but I can't sit still.
The others shush me and
tell me to sit down,
to chill out,
but I pace and talk
then laugh as the main character,
hot girl turned demon,
sinks her teeth into some jock
while Ria hides her face in a pillow and screams.

The film ends.
I snap the laptop shut.
"Right, listen,
I have a new plan."

I sketch out the gist:
it's the end of term
annual fancy rugby dinner next week.

They'll all be there.
Henry, James, all their mates.
Proud fathers, swollen
with the success of their sons.

Well, how can we ignore this opportunity
to make some noise?

THE TRUTH

"So what exactly are we going to do?
How's it going to work?"
Lori frowns.

I stand and stare out of the window
into the darkness and
whisper it,
as if that will make it
hurt
a little less.
I have to tell them.
It's time. At last.

"I did it. The post
on the website –
that first one –
it was me.
I should have told you before.
I told Ms Lark
but she gave up
and our strike didn't work
and then I was expelled.
I really messed everything up,
I'm so sorry,
but I just wanted to try to stop him.
Stop them."

I screw my eyes shut
and the girls crowd me,
stroke my hair
and my face and
touch my hands gently
and swear
it will all be okay,
they swear
they'll help me.

DECIMATION DREAM

They're cutting down the trees.

And all I can hear
above the machines
is a voice
screaming,
Hurt not the trees.

Hard to believe the girl up there is real.
Her hair flying in bunches on top of her head,
she's waving a flag
that she's made of her clothes,
standing half naked
in her bra and ripped jeans
in the rain
like it'll stop the bulldozers,
like it might stop the saws
that grate and grind,
salivating wolves,
teeth bared,
ready to tear our world, her world,
my world
to pieces.

I dream of doing
something incredible.
I dream of daring to do the impossible
sometime,
soon,
before it's too late.

RUGBY DINNER

Castle College is at its finest,
done up in Christmas best.

The halls twinkle with celebration,
boys arrive
flanked by parents,
the air bright with congratulation.

Edward, Henry, Jamie, Miles
pose for photographs beside the Christmas tree,
handsome in tuxedos,
gleaming with smiles.

Their arrival
is vivid in my imagination,
red and green and white with holly and mistletoe,

Dr March meeting and greeting,
handshakes and applause,
I can hear laughter,
the boom of it,
the slosh of wine
and clatter of cutlery,
twinkling stars of success.

They think their world is so safe.
Well now it's time for the consequence.

THE GIRLS

Camilla is Henry's date.
Lori is with Ed.
Ria and Dilly are here at home with me.

We like their photos,
posts of the boys,
the team,
champions of their league.

Lori sends an update:
Speeches soon –
you ready, Cass?

HERE WE GO

A slideshow of success.
"These young men are
our pride and joy," Dr March says
as she proceeds to congratulate
the rugby boys on their
athleticism, their strength,
team spirit and physical pre-eminence.

Parents beam,
their smiles lit with pride as the candles
twitch and shiver
and shadows dance.

We watch as Lori films live,
streaming to her stories,
gathered around my laptop,
close, breath held,
and stare as
suddenly
the screen behind Dr March
changes:

bright
white

then
full of
the
vivid truth,
the technicolour evidence
of
Castle College's
gilded
youth.

Photograph after photograph
flashes onto the screen.

Every picture Lori has ever been sent,
stored
and kept
for just such an event.

Pictures of their erect penises
followed by their threats.

Screenshots identifiable
by names and numbers that weren't deleted.

There's the silence of shock
and then outrage bursts.

Deep voices demand,
What the hell is this?

And then, I hear my voice talking over it all.

The recording plays
as I read out my own words:

last summer after our GCSEs, i was at a party (you know
those parties, where there's drinking and drugs and it's all
so much) but I felt like shit. maybe my drink was spiked,
i dunno, but i remember staggering upstairs, finding a
bedroom on my own. i thought i'd be all right. sleep it
off, this awful feeling – i couldn't stand, or see, my head
aching and my blood so heavy like i was almost dying or
something. so i lay down for a bit.
sleep,
i thought,
i'll sleep.

That very first post.
Ria and Dilly hold my hands as
I force myself to listen to my words:

and i must have passed out, cos the next thing i know
i'm kind of awake, and someone's holding my arms, while
someone pulls down my shorts and shoves

his fingers inside me.

and other things.

until someone turns off the sound.
My voice cuts out.

Lori zooms in on Dr March
who's stuttering her apologies
to the parents
as chairs scrape floors and bodies stand,
livid with rage.

Wine spills,
food is thrown.

But then the screen is back on
and Lori scans back to show
Camilla on stage
and everyone is quiet again
as she speaks into the mic.

"Wait. Please. Sit down.
This isn't a prank.
I have something to show you all tonight."

We watch as she takes off her jacket,
shows her arms to the hall,
we stare at the
livid wheels where someone has left
their mark,
then look back at the screen
and see
photos of her thighs,
dark with bruises
and
on stage,
she lifts her hair
to reveal
the fingerprints on her neck.

And then we hear the recording of Henry,
coming through the speakers,
his words loud
and clear
as he tells Camilla to take off her clothes,
to spread her legs,   that he wants sex.

And then
Camilla's reply, so quiet, so scared,
telling him,
No
over and over again.

ARRESTED

At last –
but at what cost?

Wouldn't it have been better
if they'd helped us when we first asked?

PART EIGHT

THE WOODS

"Literally nobody else cares any more,"
Dilly says.

We stand in the rain
by the charred remains of our camp
and then walk to the place
where the activists chained themselves
to the trees.

There is no one else here today.
I take a picture
and we post it.
#twopersonprotest
#wherewereyou?

The replies trickle in:
It's raining
There's a storm
My parents said it was dangerous
Go girls ...

Josh joins us,
anorak zipped right up to his chin,
hood tight round his face,

he coughs into his fist,
pale, thin
and grimacing.
"Sorry, I didn't want to give up.
Bloody weather, though, it's shite."

The three of us stand shivering and waiting and
    praying
for a reprieve
that isn't going to come.

MIGRATING

A figure comes towards us through the rain.
Slight and graceful, she moves towards us like a bird
picking her way across the earth.

I realize who it is and turn away.

"Cassie?"
Ms Lark's voice. She sounds so young.

        "What do you want?"

"To tell you I'm sorry.
I honestly tried. I did what I could."

"Well, it wasn't enough."

"I know. I know. But listen, I think you should know.
The school failed the inspection.
I just heard.
Serious breaches in safeguarding.
It means they might close, so, you know, I think
that's down to you. You should be proud."

I turn to look at her.
"What does that mean?"

"It means because what you told me wasn't handled
as it should have been that, well, heads may roll.
And I think, I hope, it won't happen again."

WEATHER

The rain pours.
We don't celebrate. We don't even smile.
Ms Lark stands with us for a while, and we don't talk.

In the end it's the weather that drives
the demolition party away,
the rain and the thunder,
the hail.
Not me,
or Dilly, Ms Lark,
or Josh.

The big burly bloke with his army of diggers
and chainsaws
tells me
not to bother coming back again,
that there's no point,
there is no chance
that we will win this one.

Dilly says,
"Screw you."
He swears under his breath
and he looks at her
like he'd like to take his machete to her neck.

WHAT DID YOU DO WITH HOPE?

We were too late.
Somehow it happened
when we turned away, our attention lost
just for a second.
Did they come in the middle of the night?
Now it is as if those trees had never been there at all.

One weekend is all it took,
a weekend when I lay in bed and slept
while the wind wrapped itself around the house.
Roots and branches, a twisted mess of intestines,
liver, heart and bowels,
are all that is left,
this
life lost,
evisceration
complete.

Gutted, I stand and stare at vacancy.
Numb, the sunshine only
catches metal, the brute bold force
of glass and steel.
Man-made,
my loss

drifts into the empty sky
on broken wings.

A car pulls up.
Grandad. Mum.
"What are you doing here, love?
Come home," she says.
She puts her arm around my waist,
and I rest my head on her shoulder which feels
stronger today.

I told her, of course, in the end
and she cried,
which is what I hadn't wanted to face.
But she believed me
and that's what matters most.

"Here," Grandad hands her a soft felt bag,
"now's a good time, I think."
Mum smiles, and dips her hand inside,
holds out a closed fist, like we're playing a game,
like I'm a little kid
and must guess to win my prize.
"Look," she says, her fingers uncurling
to reveal earth, and seeds,
"I gathered them when we were last here,

from the trees.
You can plant another forest,
Cassie, we'll do it together.
Because someone like you will always
make things grow."

ADVICE

Moira says there's always another fight.
She feeds me chocolate cake,
sticky with fudge icing,
and tells me to keep my chin up.

"At least Henry's finally facing justice,
now he's been arrested.
Gosh, Camilla's been through so much."

I nod.
The last time I saw Camilla,
last week,
we sat in silence, two cups of coffee
steaming between us,
the café a fug of heat,
a refuge from the rain outside.

I reached out and
took her hand.
We held each other, like that,
until our drinks went cold,
and then she looked at me
and I looked back,
understanding
passing like a gift beyond words.

Moira's still talking.
"And the inspection threw up a whole host of things
the school will have to fix if it wants to continue
educating our children.
That's a victory, right?
Proves that you can make a difference if you try."

"Yeah, but at what cost?
Camilla should never have suffered like that."

Dilly hugs me close.
"Come on, let's go.
We need to hurry or we'll miss the start."

I'm not sure I have the energy for this today
but everyone's expecting me
to show up,
and smile.

RAINBOW

It was raining when we set out
but once the train pulls in,
the sun is beginning to split the clouds
and somewhere
up there
is colour.

They're easy to find,
the others like us,
filling the streets with sound –
and we follow the noise like we're following a piper,
     amplified, our voices chime,
     powerful, we rhyme,
and find
     so many of us
     moving like rebellion,
     sparks bellowing into a conflagration.

So many of us.
I am doubled, echoed,
see and hear myself
repeated in the faces, smiles,
in the flames and waves.

Bodies, voices, brave
people rising up
to demand
they acknowledge our words.

I grab Dilly's hand.
We surge forward
and the river of noise
throws us up
on a wave –
we are breaking banks,
exploding dams,
refusing to be channelled into silence,
caged in airless boxes
where our voices are dampened and drowned.

Step by step, we forward march,
part of a force
that shouts
and hopes
someone will hear our words,
we make it known
that there are children being born
every second of every day
who will have to pay for our mistakes,
their fresh air poisoned by the fumes of greed,
our future choking to death on corruption.

We are the people of today and tomorrow
with skin and hair in all the colours
of all the flags of the world.

We walk and roll and lift each other –
Boudiccas, girls who do not plan on disappearing,
who refuse to ignore
hard scientific evidence that
the planet boils.

"Just don't get arrested,"
Dilly mutters,
as I jostle forwards, screaming louder
into the face of a policeman whose intruding stare
mocks us,
a reminder that we are theirs to
look at how they like.
What I wouldn't give
to make him blank,
give him eyes of stone
like Medusa
doing her best to make the point.

What I wouldn't give for the power
to petrify the men who want to touch us,
the men who are old enough

to have daughters of their own
but ogle our bodies as if they are owed.

No one's voice equals mine
as we scream our hopes to the sky
whilst the man inside Number 10,
monied,
middle-aged and
blindly deaf,
attends to the business of ignorance
and vice,
won't hear the future banging its drum
outside his office
where the only thing that matters is
the size of his profile and
the accumulating piles of power
he tries to disguise
behind the rhetoric of
doing what's right.

                                    and hobble,

                            and we walk, and hop

                    of sound

                the rainbow

            and boys,

            bright rivers of girls

        those

    I join them,

    banners flying.

    waving, waiting, cheering,

There they are – my friends,

we link arms,

brown and blonde,

caught in the rainbow's glancing light –

black, pink, green,

bunches or braids,

our faces ache with smiles –

we try again.

We swallow wind,

and fumes and

breathe in the past,

let it

fill us with intent
and purpose
which we throw
        and catch
and throw again
        to each other
as our smiles grow and strengthen.

Dilly, Lori, Ria, Camilla, Edward, Mo, Josh
and me,
we will show up and try again
and again.

I don't have to apologize
for what's happened, for who I am,
what I've done,
today and every other day
we'll fight to change
the world,
and ourselves –
we can't give up.

Dilly nudges me,
"Cassie – over there – look,"
and I stare into the rainbow,
ready to believe, for her,
in an imaginary pot of gold,

but what I see is
Grandad
and Moira
and Mum
carrying their own banner –

> we will fix the future
> for our daughters
> and sons,
> for every child
> who deserves
> the best chance.

Dilly pushes back through the crowds
and I go after her,
lighter, certain that this is a sign
that something is changing,
that after the rumble of thunder and the storm,
the frosts and the cold,
comes sun and warmth.
Together we can do better,
be more.
All is not lost.

Now,
watch us soar.

NOTE TO THE READER

There should be a zero-tolerance approach in educational settings to sexual violence and sexual harassment. It is never acceptable for anyone to feel unsafe in their school environment. In most schools safeguarding is a top priority. However, if you have experienced, or are experiencing, any of the issues raised in ACTIVIST then there are people who can help. Please reach out.

Contact Rape Crisis (England & Wales) or The Survivors Trust for details of local specialist organisations. https://rapecrisis.org.uk

The Male Survivors Partnership can provide details of services which specialise in supporting men and boys. https://malesurvivor.co.uk

NHS – Help after rape and sexual assault provides a range of advice, help and support including advice about the risk of pregnancy, sexually transmitted infections (STI), reporting to the police and forensics. https://www.nhs.uk/live-well/sexual-health/help-after-rape-and-sexual-assault/

Rape and sexual assault referral centres services can be found at: Find Rape and sexual assault referral centres.

https://www.nhs.uk/live-well/sexual-health/help-after-rape-and-sexual-assault/

Sexual assault referral centres (SARCs) offer medical, practical and emotional support. They have specially trained doctors, nurses and support workers. If children, young people, or their families are unsure which service to access, they should contact their GP or call the NHS on 111.

Childline provide free and confidential advice for children and young people.

https://www.childline.org.uk

ACKNOWLEDGEMENTS

As ever, massive thanks to Bella Pearson for her belief in my writing, and her brilliant publishing. I am so lucky to have you, Bella! My ever-supportive agents, Jessica Hare and Hilary Delamere, deserve a huge thank you for all they do. Their support means the world.

Many thanks, also, to the superstars at Guppy and Michael O'Mara who have supported the publishing of this book: Liz Scott, Hannah Featherstone, Ness Wood, Catherine Alport to name a few.

Thank you to Colyn Allsopp for type-setting so skilfully and for putting up with all my fiddly little changes, especially the rainbows!

Thanks to very dear friends and fellow writers, Amy Beashel and Alexia Casale, who have given their time and expertise so generously to help me make this book as good as it can be. Thanks also to my excellent friend Diana for her brilliant feedback and support. The north-west SCBWI gang are legends one and all; thank you to fellow YAers: Anna, Eve, Catherine, Helen, Cathy, Mel, Sumaya, Jen, Ruth, Sue and all who've critiqued and supported.

There are legions of school librarians who work tirelessly to find the right books for their readers. Thank you so much for supporting me and my work and for welcoming me into your schools.

I continue to be inspired by the many young people who are committed to making the world a better place. It has been a privilege to work with many clever, thoughtful and kind students; thanks, in particular, to the teachers and students of Loreto Grammar, Altrincham, who always put justice first.

Thank you to Yuzhen Cai for the stunning artwork and cover, and to Ness Wood for all the brilliant design.

Thank you to my dear family, in particular my mum, and my husband and daughters.

'*Gloves Off* is an intense, original and profoundly
moving verse novel, filled with the fierce, hard
joy of finding your power' *The Guardian*

'A skilful novel in blank verse . . . written with feeling,
honesty and conviction, this is a story about body
image and self-esteem that packs a knock-out punch'
Sunday Times Children's Book of the Week

'A beautiful, lyrical read. Buy it for your
daughters – and sons' *The Sun*

Lily turns sixteen with two very different sides to her life: school,
where she is badly bullied, and home with her mum and dad, warm
and comforting but with its own difficulties.

After a particularly terrible bullying incident, Lily's dad determines
to give his daughter the tools to fight back. Introducing her to
boxing, he encourages Lily to find her own worth. It is both
difficult and challenging but in confronting her own fears she finds
a way through that illuminates her life and friendships.

A page-turning and immersive YA novel in verse; a story of hope
and resilience breaking through even the most difficult situations.

AN EMPATHY DAY READ
CHOSEN FOR NATIONAL POETRY DAY
NOMINATED FOR THE CARNEGIE MEDAL

'A profoundly moving story about truth and love' **Jenny Downham**

'Beautifully brutal and devastating' **Brian Conaghan**

'After reading *Wrecked*, I am the title. Tragic, compelling, real, and beautifully written' **Teri Terry**

Sporty Joe and beautiful Imogen seem like the perfect couple on the surface. But after a tragic fatal accident, they become embroiled in a situation out of their control, and as the deception and lies at the heart of their relationship are uncovered, soon the truth is out there for all to see . . .

Structured around a dramatic and tense court case, the reader becomes both judge and jury in a stunning and page-turning novel of uncovering secrets and lies — exactly who is telling the truth?

'For fans of narrative verse and gripping quick reads, *Wrecked* by Louisa Reid is a must . . . a tense and pacey read, and like Joe, the reader is swept along in the speed of the story' *The Scotsman*

**AN EMPATHY DAY READ
CHOSEN FOR NATIONAL POETRY DAY**

Louisa Reid has spent most of her life reading. And when she's not doing that she's writing stories, or imagining writing them at least. An English teacher, her favourite part of the job is sharing her love of reading and writing with her pupils.

Louisa writes about things that she thinks are important to young people, and all people generally, really. Drawn to write about themes of female empowerment and personal freedom, GLOVES OFF is about bullying and body image, with some boxing thrown in too. Louisa hopes the novel will strike a chord with anyone who's ever had to fight for self-confidence and self-belief – things which are, for many, very hard won.

Louisa lives with her family in the north-west of England and is proud to call a place near Manchester home.

GUPPY
BOOKS

Guppy Books is an independent children's publisher based in Oxford in the UK, publishing exceptional fiction for children of all ages. Small and responsive, inclusive and communicative, Guppy Books was set up in 2019 and publishes only the very best authors and illustrators from around the world.

From brilliantly funny illustrated tales for five-year-olds to inspiring and thought-provoking novels for young adults, Guppy Books promises to publish something for everyone. If you'd like to know more about our authors and books, go to the Guppy Aquarium on YouTube where you'll find interviews, drawalongs and all sorts of fun.

We hope that our books bring pleasure to young people of all ages, and also to the adults sharing these books with them. Children's literature plays a part in giving both young and old the resources and reflection needed to grow up in today's ever-changing world, and we hope that you enjoy this small piece of magic!

Bella Pearson
Publisher

www.guppybooks.co.uk